Falling for a Furry

I0660235

By Jay Thornton

A GOSHEN PUBLISHERS BOOK   VIRGINIA

Jay Thornton

Falling for a Furry

ISBN: 978-1-7342639-7-8

Library of Congress Cataloging-in-Publication Data

Published in 2021 by:

GOSHEN PUBLISHERS LLC
P.O. Box 1562
Stephens City, Virginia, USA
www.GoshenPublishers.com

Our books may be purchased in bulk for promotional, educational, or business use. For inquiries please contact the publisher via email: Agents@GoshenPublishers.com.

First Edition 2021

Cover designed by Goshen Publishers LLC

Printed in the United States of America

Introduction

Taciana: "Hello! I'm Taciana! And I'm so excited you've found this book."

Jackson: "Several thousand years in the future, this is how books are written. Computers take the events that happen and create the text to share. To save paper and prevent waste, it's written with the speaker's name first."

Taciana: "Right! So it might be a little bit strange for you at first, but you'll get the hang of it. This style doesn't talk as much about the settings or what people look like. It allows you to use your imagination to make us look however you want us to look!"

Jackson: "I really hope you enjoying learning a little about me-"

Serena: "And me!"

Ramona: "I'm the most important one!"

Tawny: "Boy, you wish!"

Taciana: "Quiet, you three! This isn't your story. It's mine and Jackson's."

Jackson: "But don't worry, you three are in here plenty, too."

Taciana: "We hope you enjoy our story! This is the first time anyone's learned about what it's like to be a furry teenager in Glassbec, so I'm excited to find out what you think."

Jackson: "Lights...camera...action!"

A Fateful Meeting

The planet Earth has gone through much ever since the war of 3020 between the humans and the furries. The furries won against the humans with strategically minded attacks, using teamwork, whereas the humans used brute force, thus resulting in their downfall. The race of humans died out. Well, all except for one teenage boy who was jettisoned into space by his parents before the furry army overran the planet and finished the remaining humans off, banishing them to a small area for their misdeeds and abuse of their planet and people. As time has passed, the furries have colonized every corner of the planet and there are no more humans. There are also no more problems, the kinds humans had created on what was their former planet. In fact, the furries have not only made the planet healthier and cleaner, being of a caring nature and teamwork minded, they all do their best to help each other.

.......Two-Thousand Years Later.......

The stasis pod containing the boy slowly drifts back into Earth's surprisingly cleaner atmosphere and forcefully lands on the outskirts of a town called Glassbec. The town awakens to the loud vibrations of the crash and the inhabitants feel compelled to investigate, rushing out of their homes. One of the locals, a beautiful teenage rabbit furry, comes closer and wonders how to open the strange device.

Rabbit Furry Girl: "Such an unusual device."

Mother Rabbit Furry: "Taciana, don't touch anything. We don't know what that object is."

Taciana: "Mom, it's only a stasis pod and looks to be thousands of years old. This could contain treasures from the past. Oh look, a button!"

With a hiss, the pod opens, revealing something none of the onlookers ever thought possible.

Taciana: "My goodness, is that what I think it is?"

Mrs. Rabeau: "Taciana Rabeau! What did I just say?"

Taciana: "Mom, relax. It's nothing dangerous. In fact, it actually looks like a human."

Griggs: "A human? I'm taking him in for questioning."

Taciana: "No, please, Mr. Griggs. I know you're a part of a great line of war veterans, but don't hurt him. He looks harmless."

Griggs: "Humans were the reason why this world was so screwed up from the very beginning. They are the reason why it took us so long to change the world for the better, young Taciana."

Taciana: "But this might be the last human in existence. We cannot just toss him away like he's nothing. He's an endangered species. This also might be our chance to educate him."

During the conversation the human teenage boy awakens from stasis and startles, seeing furries standing around him. Fearful and confused, he starts backing away. His legs are wobbly from being in stasis and he doesn't go far.

Taciana: "Wait! I just want to talk to you! Come back! Look, I'm not a threat. I just want to talk and maybe get to know you better, that's all."

Teenage Boy: "Alright, then start talking."

Taciana: "My name is Taciana Rabeau. What is yours?"

Teenage Boy: "Okay, Taciana, I go by the name of Jackson Le Tontione."

Taciana: "I've never seen a human before."

Jackson: "I gotta find a way back home. I don't know where I am."

Taciana: "Um, I don't think you have a home anywhere because no one has seen a human in over two thousand years."

Jackson: "No, that's not possible."

Taciana: "Yes, it's true. Your kind doesn't exist anymore. Wait, don't be sad. Come on, you can come stay with me and my family."

Jackson: "Are you sure about that, Taciana? I just feel like my presence isn't welcome here. Everyone is staring at me and pointing."

Taciana: "I will make sure you are welcomed with open arms. Follow me, it's not far."

The two walk together to the family's large house and are greeted by Taciana's three sisters and her older brother, who had been watching through a window.

Tawny: "Tacci's back! Oh snap, who is the handsome human she bought?"

Ramona: "Oh my goodness, I get to touch his muscles first!"

Serena: "I want him!"

Taciana: "First of all, I found Jackson outside in a stasis pod, and second, please give him some space, everyone. He's not a pet. Humans have feelings too."

Serena: "Hmph, I just wanted to get to know my Jackson better."

Ramona: "Excuse me!?"

Tawny: "I saw him walk in the door first!"

Warrick: "Look, little sisters, just let the dude have some elbow room."

Jackson: "Thanks. It's good to meet you all."

Warrick: "No problem, my human brother from another mother."

The parents, Mr. and Mrs. Rabeau, come down and are surprised at seeing a human boy in their home. Looking uncomfortable with having a human in his home, the father decides to kick Jackson out. He raises his foot when Taciana intervenes.

Taciana: "Daddy, please don't kick Jackson out. He only needs a place to stay for the night."

Mr. Rabeau: "Hmm okay, but for one night only and out he goes."

Mrs. Rabeau: "Don't worry dear, we will let him stay in the guest cottage until we find someone who will adopt him."

Taciana: "Come on, Jackson. I'll show you to the guest cottage. It's actually pretty big."

The two walk through the house, Taciana pointing out rooms as they go, until they reach a door that leads to the outside. The two climb up an incredibly long hill.

Jackson: "Whew. That's quite a walk."

Taciana: "Well, here we are. This is your new home."

Jackson: "Wow, this is a guest cottage?"

Taciana: "What can I say? My folks like making guests feel at home."

Jackson stares in wonder. The cottage has a bedroom, a small kitchen, a bathroom, and a living room. There's a TV, a refrigerator filled with snacks, and a computer sitting on a small desk. As Jackson looks around, he suddenly stops.

Jackson: "I forgot to thank you for releasing me from stasis."

Taciana: "You're welcome, Jackson. Well, I should probably head for my room now, since it's almost time for bed. Goodnight."

Jackson: "Right. Goodnight, Tacia."

Jackson uses the guest cottage computer for a while, researching all that had happened in the last few thousand years. He is surprised at how much the furries had done, and even though he misses his family and other humans, he is glad to be out of the cramped stasis pod.

A New Day

As the sun rose above the Rabeau household, sending down golden rays filtering through tree tops and glittering on the ground below, Jackson woke up, the sun shining in his eyes. For a moment he forgot where he was, then he remembered. He also remembered Taciana saying something about how he'd have to go to school, because every young furry went to school until they reached adulthood. There was a knock on the door.

Taciana: "Jackson?"

Jackson: "Come in. Such a peaceful morning. Even the air outside this window smells wonderful. This is such an incredible moment to savor."

Taciana: "Why don't you come have breakfast in the main house?"

Jackson: "Okay."

As Jackson and Taciana get closer, he can hear Taciana's sisters arguing in the kitchen while they eat breakfast.

Ramona: "So true."

Tawny: "Not true."

Serena: "Is too!"

Jackson: "What are you all arguing over?"

Warrick: "They are arguing over who gets to go out with you. They still want to parade you around like a pet. But Taciana told them you are going out with her now."

Taciana: "That's right. It doesn't matter what you three think, because he already asked me out to have dinner and a movie."

Warrick: (whispers) "Taciana is my favorite little sister, she's very committed and she hates it when other girls stand in the way. So don't ever betray her."

Jackson: "Got it."

Warrick: "Also, we managed to persuade our parents to let you stay here as long as you like."

Jackson: "Thanks, bro. I was a little nervous about who might want to adopt me."

Warrick: "No problem.

Taciana: "Okay, guys, we have to get ready for school. Jackson, Mom got you enrolled so you'll come with us. I can't wait to share with you all of the things we do here. I wonder if any are the same like you used to do."

The three sisters grab their bookbags and walk outside. Taciana takes Jackson's hand and leads him to Warrick's truck where the others are waiting. Serena, Ramona, and Tawny are pouting.

Jackson: "Well this is going to be a long, but interesting day."

Warrick: "Alright, everyone ready? Time to ride!"

Furry High School

Warrick drives down the street towards the school. Jackson's eyes are glued to the window as he stares at the new scenery. While many things look the same, he notices almost everyone is smiling and helping each other. The city is clean, and even the cars drive without putting out puffs of black smoke. He glances around inside the car. The little sisters are still upset, and Taciana is going over her homework one more time. Jackson tries to break the silence by getting to know Warrick better.

Jackson: "Nice ride, Warrick."

Warrick: "Thanks. It is a 5018 Range Rover Evoque. My pride and joy."

Jackson: "Cool. You think I could get a car at some point?"

Warrick: "Sure dude, in fact, here is some cash for the new car of your choice. I figured you might need it, being new here and all."

Jackson: "Thanks, bro. You are awesome!"

Warrick: "No problem, just hide the cash inside the secret compartment of your locker."

Jackson: "Lockers have secret compartments in this school?"

Warrick: "Sure, in fact we are halfway there. You'll see it soon."

Taciana: "Sorry to interrupt this interesting conversation, but I need to have a talk with Jackson."

Warrick: "Say what you have to say, Tacci. We are all right here."

Taciana: "Okay, fine. Jackson, I don't think you should be driving a car on your own so soon."

Jackson: "Why not?"

Taciana: "The thing is… you're a human and some furries are not going to like the fact of seeing someone of your species behind the wheel."

Jackson: "Taciana, are you saying I should worry about speciesism in your school?"

Taciana: "Yes, that's what I am saying, Jackson."

Jackson: "I can prove to them that it doesn't matter what species you are in order to get along with others."

Ramona: "That is deep and pure of you to say, Jackson."

Warrick makes a sharp turn and stops quickly in his personal parking spot close to the school's front entrance. They all get out of the truck, and Warrick locks the doors behind them. Jackson stares up at the building in front of them. It looked like he remembered school to be. A large brick building with trees on the outside. There were picnic benches scattered around, a long sidewalk, and lots, and lots of species of furries, all starting their day.

Warrick: "Welcome to Wild Eye High School!"

Taciana: "Are you ready for your first day here?"

Jackson: "Absolutely."

Serena: "Come on, Jackson. I'll give you a quick tour before class starts."

Tawny: "I should give the tour."

Ramona: "No, it should be me because I barely had a chance to speak to him!"

Taciana: "Alright you three, that is enough. Go to class and I will lead him in, okay? Come on, Warrick. Time for class."

Warrick: "Alright sis, I'll go. Don't worry, Renet, I'll see you later after school."

Renet: "Sure thing, sugar. Hi Taciana, who is this?"

Taciana: "Hey, Renet. This is Jackson, and he's newly enrolled here at Wild Eye. He's also staying in our guest cottage for a while."

Jackson: "Nice to meet you, Renet. So you are Warrick's girlfriend?"

Renet: "Yes. Hello! Wow, I did not know you had a new gentleman living with you, Tacci."

Taciana: "Yeah, it's more like he found me."

Taciana and Renet show Jackson around to his classes. On the way, they run into Carina Fox.

Carina: "Hey, there are my favorite rabbits! How are you all doing?"

Taciana: "It is going great, Carina. We are just showing the newbie around before the first round of classes begins."

Carina: "A human? Wow! What's your name, handsome?"

Jackson: "Call me Jackson Tontione.

Carina: "You want to call me sometime?"

Jackson: "Maybe so, just lay your number on me."

Carina: "You are so cute! Here is my number. Call me sometime okay J.T.?"

Carina blows a kiss in his direction as she walks off to her first class.

Taciana: "What was that?"

Jackson: "Oh come on, Taciana. I was just having a little fun."

Taciana: "I don't like other girls flirting with you."

Jackson: "The thing is, you have not marked me as a mate, therefore, I am fair game to any girl who wants to see me."

Taciana: "Fine, let's just go to class."

Renet: "Unfortunately, he is right, bestie."

Taciana: "Yeah, I know. I just want him to myself and not have to share him with anyone."

After everyone got to their first classes, Jackson realizes that none of the Rabeaus are in his. The rest of the day, furries of all different species stare, eyeballing him due to his appearance.

........Seven hours later........

Jackson: "Well, I am glad that's over."

Sophia Wolfe: "I'll say. Some days it feels like a prison. Yet it is always important to learn something new."

Jackson: "Very true indeed. Who might you be; if you don't mind my asking?"

Sophia Wolfe: "My name is Sophia Wolfe. I'm one of the most popular girls in school."

Jackson: "It is a pleasure to meet you. I am known as Jackson Le Tontione, the one and only human in town."

Sophia: "So I hear. You want to maybe go swimming sometime? There's a big pool in town."

Jackson: "Sure. It will be my treat once I purchase my new car."

Sophia: "Oh really? Which one are you planning to buy?"

Jackson: "I'll surprise you. I'm not really sure just yet, but it's going to be great."

Sophia: "Ooooh, fancy I can't wait."

Jackson and Sophia smile at each other while Taciana, who is walking towards Warrick's truck, watches the two getting too close, jealousy riddled all over her face. As Sophia walks off, giving Jackson her number, Taciana comes up.

Taciana: "I told you that you are my man, and no one's toy. Don't let me catch you intentionally being overly friendly with other girls again because it really hurts me when you do."

Jackson: "I am sorry, Tacci. I never realized your feelings were that strong for me."

Taciana: "It's fine, it's just I am in love with you and I want us to be more than friends."

Jackson: "That is fine with me, Taciana."

Taciana: "I wanted you for myself ever since I freed you from that stasis pod."

Jackson: "Well, I kind of fell for those gorgeous blue eyes of yours."

Taciana: "You're so cheesy, but I love it. Come on, we will just wait at Warrick's truck for the others."

New Car

Jackson: "You wanna come with me while we get my new car?"

Taciana: "Sure, my family and I know how to manage money."

Jackson: "Is that why everyone in class says that your family is rich?"

Taciana: "Yeah, kind of. But we are not millionaires."

Jackson: "Billionaires?"

Taciana: "Yeah, we are billionaires. Our parents work extremely hard to maintain that status. Plus, we donate thousands of dollars every year to help charities around the world. In fact, our school is doing a big project next week where we are going to be building homes for the furries who aren't as well off as others are. It's called Flats for Furries. My parents donated the supplies for it. It's going to be fun, you should come with us."

Jackson: "Wow, you have a big heart, Tacci."

Taciana: "Well, we try."

Jackson: "I've never built a house before."

Taciana: "That's okay! There's a job for everyone."

Warrick walks in after saying goodbye to Renet and settles in the driver's seat.

Warrick: "Hey, you two."

Jackson and Taciana: "Hey."

Jackson: "So anyways, are we going to get my new car?"

Warrick: "Yes, indeed."

Then they spot the other three Rabeau sisters coming to the truck in a hurry.

Serena: "It is mine, Ramona!"

Ramona: "No, mine, Serena!"

Tawny: "Excuse me, but it is obviously mine!"

The three continue arguing until Taciana blows her conflict whistle.

Serena: "What was that for, Taciana?"

Taciana: "It was the only way to get you to stop fighting."

Ramona: "It hurts my ears, sister."

Tawny: "Yeah."

Taciana: "We are all here because Jackson is going to buy a new car and we need to support him on what he chooses. No arguing, you three."

Jackson: "Thank you, Tacci."

Warrick: Alright everyone, settle down we are on our way to the dealership.

Tawny: "So Jackson, what kind of ride did you have in mind?"

Jackson: "I will let you know when the purchase of the car is complete on the way out."

..........A Short Time Later..........

Jackson is strolling around the lot looking at the different cars. A young sales assistant comes out from behind the service desk to help. She walks up to Jackson and shakes his hand.

Sales Assistant: "Good afternoon and welcome to Leopard Auto!"

Jackson: "Hello there, who do I have the pleasure of addressing?"

Sales Assistant: "My name is Riley Polecat and I know who you are, Jackson Tontione."

Jackson: "Really? I guess word travels fast."

Riley: "Actually, I go to the same school as you."

Jackson: "Oh well, then I guess you could give me a discount."

Riley: "You are cute and funny."

Jackson: "Well, I try."

Riley: "So what is your style of car, Mr. Tontione?"

Jackson: "The car I am looking to purchase is a black 5020 Leopard F-Type."

Riley: "Okay, follow me. Here is our newest 5020 Leopard F-Type model at a good price."

Jackson: "Awesome!!! This is the one."

Riley: "Excellent choice."

Jackson: "What is the cost of the vehicle?"

Riley: "The floor-plan price for this one is precisely one hundred thousand and six hundred dollars."

Jackson: "Woah, that is pretty steep."

Riley: "Tell you what, having a human drive one of our cars would be good advertising. I'll cut the monthly payment for the car which is normally seven fifty and make it half, which means you will be paying only three hundred and seventy-five dollars per month. Plus, I will sell the vehicle to you for only fifty thousand and three hundred dollars if you take me out for a few dates."

Jackson: "That is very generous of you Riley, but I already have a girlfriend waiting outside."

Riley: "Can she do this?"

Jackson: "How did you pull that paper out of my pocket?"

Riley: "Magicians do not reveal the secret behind the trick, Mr. Suave, and we can split a batch of cooked mice and fish."

Jackson: "Riley, you're very pretty for a polecat, but I don't think that is a good idea. But I heard the school will be building homes for furries soon, maybe I'll see you there."

Riley: "Okay, Jackson. I had to try! I've always wanted to date a human. See you in school!"

Riley and Jackson wave at each other. Jackson grabs the keys and the vehicle paperwork to take with him.

Jackson: "Let's ride!"

Taciana: "Mind if I join you?"

Jackson: "Not at all, Tacci. Hop in!"

The two drive off with Warrick's truck following behind them all the way home.

Fireflies

Jackson: "Hey Taciana, can I ask you a question?"

Taciana: "What is it?"

Jackson: "Do you still want to go out on our date tonight?"

Taciana: "Actually, Jackson, could we have our date next Saturday instead?"

Jackson: "Awww, why my beautiful bunny?"

Taciana: "This beautiful bunny has a lot of homework and so do you, my strong man."

Jackson: "Can I at least have a smooch before we have to go to bed, Tacci?"

Taciana: "Okay. Mmmmwwwah. Was that better, big man?"

Jackson: "Oh yeah."

Taciana: "Do you need help with your homework? We can do it together!"

Jackson: "It is a deal."

.......Eight Hours Later.......

Everyone was fast and sound asleep in their designated rooms. A pebble hits the side of the window of the guest cottage, causing Jackson to wake up.

Jackson: "Aaaaaaah. What the heck was that?"

Sophia: "Hey Jacky, it's me, Sophia Wolfe."

Jackson: "Sophia?"

Sophia: "I was wondering if we could take a stroll by the pond real quick."

Jackson: "Okay sure. But isn't this a little risky considering Taciana claimed me as her mate?"

Sophia: "Come on, Jackson, didn't humans have a sense of adventure in your time?"

Jackson: "Well, yeah, but not this late at night. I'm tired."

Sophia: "Come on, it will be fun."

Jackson: "Alright, we will go, but I have to be back before the others wake up."

Sophia: "Yes! Use the trampoline I brought. It's below you."

Jackson jumps down from the bedroom window and lands on the trampoline. Sophia leads Jackson to the pond, where fireflies illuminate the area.

Jackson: "Sophia, this place is spot on."

Sophia: "Yes, I love to come here. I often dance with the fireflies. Would you care for a dance?"

Jackson: "A dance by a pond?"

Sophia: "Why not?"

Jackson: "I am just not used to dancing. People always laughed at me whenever I tried."

Sophia: "I can teach you how."

Jackson: "Really?"

Sophia: "I sure can. I even have music."

Jackson: "Is that an automated stereo?"

Sophia: "Why, yes it is."

As the two start to dance, Jackson doing quite badly and Sophia giggling at him, they are unaware that they are being watched until Sophia hears something and pulls away, looking around with worry in her eyes.

Sophia: "Jackson? Did you hear the rustling in those bushes over there?"

Jackson: "A little bit, but don't worry so much. It is probably just the wind."

Sophia: "Will you protect me if it turns out to be something dangerous?"

Jackson: "Of course, Sophie. I promise you that.

Onlooker: "That traitorous witch. She will pay dearly for cheating on me."

Fireflies: Part 2

Onlooker: "I cannot believe this!"

The onlooker captures video footage of Jackson and Sophia for a few minutes before running back home in anger.

Sophia: "What do you want to do now, J.T.?"

Jackson: "Can I see where you live?"

Sophia: "Sure! My house isn't as big as Taciana's, but I like it."

The two walk to Sophia's house.

Sophia: "Okay my folks are sleeping, so is my little sister, so we will have to be very quiet."

Jackson: "Sophia, these are some nice digs."

Voice: "Sophie?"

Sophia: "Uhoh, it is my little sister, Tia."

Tia: "Are you alright in there Sophie?"

Sophia: "I'm fine."

Tia: "Who is that?"

Sophia: "Tia, this is my friend Jackson and he was helping me study."

Tia: "You were making a lot of noise and it woke me up."

Sophia: "Sorry. You should go back to sleep."

Tia: "Okay, but I'm a little scared of the dark."

Sophia: "Hey, how about we tell you a story."

Tia: "Really?"

Sophia: "Yes, of course."

Tia: "Yeah!"

Sophia: "On a dark and stormy night, there lived a beautiful girl named Tulcania, and she met a boy who wanted to show her the world through a different view."

Tia: "Is the girl a wolf?"

Sophia: "Yes, she was a wolf furry and the boy was not of this world, but a survivor from another."

Tia: "What happened next?"

Sophia: "Jackson, you wanna tell her?"

Jackson: "The boy took her to a special place where the spirits of light dance in the sky. As they watched the Northern lights, Tulcania told the boy how she really felt and they shared a tender moment together. Then the rest is to be continued."

Tia: "Aww, please tell me how it ends."

Sophia: "The two lovers stared into each other's eyes until they saw the great spirit of light descend upon the boy and turn him into the wolf of Tulcania's dreams. The spirit gave him a new name, Uruq, for his new furry form, and they both lived in peace for the rest of their days."

Tia: "Thank you for telling me that story, guys. It was amazing."

Sophia: "You're very welcome, Tia. Now, it's time to go to sleep."

Tia: "Okay, but I wanna ask about the spirits of light."

Sophia: "Sure sweetheart, what about them?"

Tia: "Are they real?"

Sophia: "Yes, yes they are."

Jackson: "For real?"

Sophia: "Absolutely. In fact, I can show you where they often meet in our world."

Jackson: "I will take you up on that offer, wolfie."

Sophia: "It's a date then."

Tia: "Are you two going to be together like Tulcania and Uruq?"

Sophia and Jackson: "Goodnight, Tia."

Tia: "Goodnight, Sophie. Goodnight, Mr. Jackson."

Ambush

A new sunny morning rises above Glassbec. Still asleep, Sophia is startled by a knock on her bedroom door. She rushes to it and opens it, but only a crack. She and Jackson had fallen asleep talking and he was still in her room.

Mrs. Wolfe: "Sophia?"

Sophia: "Good morning, Ma."

Mrs. Wolfe: "Is there someone else in there with you?"

Sophia: "What? No, it is just me and little Tia. She got scared so I told her a story last night. She fell asleep and I couldn't move her back."

Mrs. Wolfe: "Are you sure? I heard another voice coming from your room when I got up for a glass of water."

Sophia: "It was an audiobook."

Mrs. Wolfe: "Are you telling the truth?"

Sophia: "Okay, I snuck my friend in and we both fell asleep."

Mrs. Wolfe: "A human?"

Sophia: "Yes."

Mrs. Wolfe: "You know your father and I would not approve of this."

Sophia: "I know Dad has his view of humans, but Jackson is different."

Mrs. Wolfe: "He is not a furry and you should not be alone with him, period."

Sophia: "Jackson actually cares about me and Tia like he would if his own family was here."

Mrs. Wolfe: "What happened to you and Bruno? I thought you were with him."

Sophia: "Bruno doesn't even care about where I go or about my feelings, because he is too busy with his extracurricular activities to call or chat with me. Jackson actually took the time to get to know me. But I'm not going out with him. He already has a girlfriend. Taciana."

Mr. Wolfe: "Sophia Wolfe, why is there a human boy in your room?"

Sophia: "Daddy, please don't hurt him!"

Mr. Wolfe: "We specifically forbade you from sneaking anyone in the house without our approval!"

Jackson and Tia wake up from the yelling.

Jackson: "Sophie, what's with the shouting?"

Tia: "Morning, Mommy and Daddy."

Mr. Wolfe: "Hey honey, did you sleep well?"

Tia: "Yeah, Mr. Jackson helped Sophia tell me a good story last night."

Mr. Wolfe: "Really?"

Tia: "Yup."

Mrs. Wolfe: "Why don't you head downstairs? You too, Sophia."

Sophia: "Come on, Tia."

Tia: "What will happen to Mr. Jackson?"

Sophia: "He will be okay as long as Dad doesn't kick him out."

Mrs. Wolfe follows them downstairs to give them their breakfast, while Mr. Wolfe stays in the room and speaks with Jackson.

Mr. Wolfe: "So, a human, eh?"

Jackson: "Yes, sir."

Mr. Wolfe: "I am not necessarily supporting this at all, Jackson. You humans had a bad reputation. You nearly destroyed this place."

Jackson: "I overheard the conversation while I was trying to sleep. I would never hurt Sophia at all and I would do anything to prove it."

Mr. Wolfe: "There is one way to prove you are worthy of my trust."

Jackson: "Really? What is it?"

Mr. Wolfe: "You have to become a furry."

Jackson: "Fair deal, Mr. Wolfe. Where do I have to go to turn into one?"

Mr. Wolfe: "The process will have to take place on the sacred mountain of light."

Jackson: "Alright, I will do it."

Mr. Wolfe: "Good lad. Now let's head down."

The two head downstairs to join the others in the kitchen.

Sophia: "Hey Jacky, I have one last piece of bacon. Wanna share?"

Jackson: "Sure."

Tia: "Sister?"

Sophia: "What is on your mind, Tia?"

Tia: "Does Jackson have a home?"

Sophia: "Yes, he lives with our neighbors, the Rabeaus."

Jackson: "Oh right, I have to go back to the Rabeau's guest house."

Sophia: "Call me later, J.T."

.......A Few Minutes Later.......

As Jackson is walking back to the Rabeau's house, a group of three furries including a wolf, coyote and a bear follow then surround him.

Jackson: "What's up guys?"

Louie Coyote: "What's going on here is that Bruno wants to talk."

Cyprus Bear: "Yeah, human."

Bruno Sullivan: "Jackson Tontione, right?"

Jackson: "Yeah and who's asking?"

Bruno: "Name's Bruno Sullivan."

Jackson: "What do you want with me?"

Bruno: "He asked about what I want. Isn't that funny, boys? What I want is for you to stop seeing my girlfriend Sophia, fool. You feel me?"

Jackson: "I don't know what you are talking about."

Bruno: "Don't even play that card! I caught you two on tape by the pond together."

Jackson: "If you really cared about her, then maybe she wouldn't have come to me."

Bruno: "You human scum!"

Jackson: "You will have to be quicker than that."

Bruno: "Say goodnight, human!"

The two fight. Jackson is evading Bruno, but finally Bruno trips Jackson. As he sprawls on the ground, Sophia rushes up, running to help Jackson.

Sophia: "Bruno, stop!"

Bruno: "Get out of my way, Sophia! How could you do this to me?"

Sophia: "I guess I see how you really are, you jerk! Jackson and I are just friends. Jackson! Are you alright?"

Jackson: "I am fine Sophie."

Sophia: "I will take care of Bruno, while you head back to Taciana's house."

Jackson: "You got it."

Bruno: "Oh, I'm going to turn him into mincemeat!"

Sophia: "That's enough Bruno. I have already moved on from you."

She takes the camera with the video footage of her and Jackson and crushes it to pieces.

Bruno: "That was my best camera!"

Sophia: "Then you should've taken better care of it."

Bruno: "You are really choosing that human for a friend over me?"

Sophia: "Yes I am. Do you know why, Bruno?"

Bruno: "Why?"

Sophia: "Jackson actually cares about me, listens to my problems, offers good advice, and wanted to know the real me the moment I met him. Plus, I am done with your overly violent behavior. Not to mention you are spending too much of your time after school on things other than me!"

Bruno: "Come on, Soph. I just wanted to surprise you this weekend."

Sophia: "Oh, so now I'm suddenly more important than your sports tryouts, after ignoring me for five weeks?"

Bruno: "I was busy working on getting a track scholarship!"

He shoves her to the ground angrily. Sophia picks herself up off the ground and brushes the dirt off of her dress. Bruno offers his hand to help her up.

Bruno: "Soph, I didn't mean to do that. Come on, you know me."

Sophia: "If this is how you treat others, then I say we're done."

Bruno: "Whatever. I am out of here. Let's go, boys. But all you goody-goodys are going to regret it. You'll see. Me and the boys have a plan."

Wild Eye Fox

After Jackson takes a shower, he heads back to the bedroom to change and puts on a new t-shirt with a lightning bolt on it. It's another beautiful day so he goes outside onto the soft green lawn.

Jackson: "Alright, now it is time to do fifty early morning push-ups to ensure my toughness. Oh yeah, Jackson is on the prowl."

Ramona: "Good morning."

Jackson: "Good morning to you too, Ramona. How'd you sleep?"

Ramona: "I'm alright. I just couldn't help but notice those muscles of yours."

Jackson: "Thanks. So, why are you so gussied up?"

Ramona: "I wanted to see if it would impress you. Do you like my outfit?"

Jackson: "Yeah, it looks nice. Did you find someone special two days ago?"

Ramona: "I actually have."

Jackson: "That's good news! Who is it?"

Ramona: "I'm looking at him."

Jackson: "Look, Ramona, I have already chosen Taciana and my choice has not changed."

Ramona: "I don't care."

Jackson: "Ramona, you are a very pretty girl, but I am not betraying her."

Ramona: "You really think I'm pretty?"

Jackson: "Yes, but we should not be doing this now."

Ramona: "I am not going to give up on you."

Taciana: "Ramona, get off of him!"

Jackson: "Thanks, Taciana."

Taciana: "No problem, big man. Hope the rest of your day won't involve my sisters trying to make a move on you."

Ramona: "Hmph, why did you interrupt us?"

Taciana: "I stopped you because he's only faithful to me. Anyways, I have some new breakfast ideas. Do you want to join me?"

Jackson: "Hang on, I'm getting a text message."

Carina: "Hi Jackson, could you help me study for my upcoming biology quiz on Monday?"

Jackson: "Sure Tacci, I would be more than happy to help you make a new sort of breakfast. Then it looks like Carina needs help to study for a quiz. So, what do you have in mind, beautiful?"

Taciana: "How about pancakes with mixed berries in them?"

Jackson: "That sounds really good."

The three go to the kitchen to make breakfast. While there, Taciana talks about their Flats for Furries project.

Jackson: "Mhhm. Yeah. Sounds great."

Taciana: Jacky, are you focused on me talking or me making breakfast?"

Jackson: "Actually, I'm focusing on a beautiful bunny who can do it all."

Ramona: "Blech! I am going to be sick if you two start making out."

Taciana: "Stop being so jealous and wake everyone up, okay Ramona? Breakfast is served!"

Jackson: "It sure looks good."

Ramona: "Give me a freaking break."

Taciana: "I'm sorry, Jacky. Please disregard my sister's childish complaints at the table."

Jackson: "Don't worry, Tacci, I understand. Little sisters. Well anyways, I have to go to Carina's to help her study for her biology class. You can tell me more about the Flats for Furries later, okay?"

Taciana: "Well, okay. Just make sure you listen next time. It's a really important project. And about Carina, I have offered to tutor her before but she has said no every time."

Jackson: "There is only one possibility, Taciana. She obviously has a thing for me."

Taciana: "Don't joke about that, Jacky. I don't want to lose you to anyone."

Jackson: "It will be fine, Tacci, nothing is going to happen. Okay?"

Taciana: "Okay, you can go. Just help my best friend because otherwise she will be retaking the class."

Jackson: "It is going to work out."

A short time later, Jackson pulls up to Carina's house.

Jackson: "Alright, I'm here now. No need to be nervous. Just be yourself and teach her what you know."

Carina: "Hey Jackson, I am so glad you're here."

Jackson: "What did you need help with?"

Carina: "I have a biology quiz in a couple of days and I need help figuring out this last question."

Jackson: "Let me see your homework. Well, it says to define what a scientific name of a species is and to give an example of one."

Carina: "Is that like Latin?"

Jackson: "Almost, except it is actually known as a binomial name."

Carina: "Oh okay. Now it all makes sense. Thank you, Jackson, I really appreciate it."

Jackson: "You're welcome, Carina. Is there anything else I can help you with?"

Carina: "Nope, that was all I needed."

Jackson: "Great. I guess I will see you on Monday."

Carina: "Wait! I want to show you something."

Jackson: "Okay. What is it?"

Carina: "It is the spot where the spirits dance in the sky. I was wondering if you wanted to come and watch them with me after dark?"

Jackson: "Sure, sounds interesting. Does something special happen there?"

Carina: "It is the one place where you could change into a furry."

Jackson: "Sophia and her dad told me a similar story. I almost thought it wasn't real."

Carina: "Jackson, it's very real."

Jackson: "That's interesting, but I have to head out."

Carina: "Wait! Can you stay with me, please?"

Jackson: "Carina, I know very few furries accept humans, but I doubt your folks would agree."

Carina: "But you'll regret it if you don't see it. Let's go!"

Jackson and Carina go on a long walk towards the spirit hill of light and see spirits of all sizes coming together in a harmonic circle at the very peak.

Carina: "It is the most beautiful sight to see here in Glassbec. Most furry couples actually come to the top of this hill for special moments. If you know what I mean."

Jackson: "I get you. Whew, we are finally at the top. What do I need to do to become a furry?"

Carina: "First, you must ask the spirits for permission before they can grant your request."

Jackson: "Great spirits of light, I humbly ask to lend me your ear."

The light suddenly lowers down to his level and it brightens a little to let Jackson know he has their attention.

The Lead Spirit: "What is your request, young human?"

Jackson: "My request is to become a dhole furry."

The Lead Spirit: "Are you at peace with your decision?"

Jackson: "I am, great spirit."

The Lead Spirit: "Very well. Remember, you cannot change back once you make this choice."

Jackson: "I understand."

The spirits then surround Jackson entirely and slowly change him into his desired form.

As the spirits complete Jackson's transformation, they return upwards above the hilltop.

Carina: "Jackson?"

Jackson: "Whoa. How do I look?"

Carina: "Furry."

Jackson: "Hehehe, thanks. Anyways it is getting late I better go. Boy, I'm going to surprise everyone!"

Destiny

The very next morning Jackson opens his eyes up to the sun's rays beaming down on his eyes through the window. Jackson's new smartphone phone rings with Taciana's photo on the screen.

Jackson: "Hey, Tacci!"

 Taciana: "Morning, handsome. I woke up early and wondered how the studying went.

Jackson: "I think she understands everything for her quiz."

Taciana: "Well, thanks for teaching her, I really appreciate you helping one of my best friends."

Jackson: "Not a problem, sweetheart."

Taciana: "Now come on to the house. I have a surprise for you."

Jackson: "Okay, I look forward to it. I'll see you there."

A short time later, Jackson enters the kitchen door of the

main house.

Jackson: "Taciana?"

Taciana: "Up here Jackson!"

Jackson walks upstairs to her room and sees that she's in her swimsuit posing.

Taciana: "Oh my! What happened to you, Jacky?"

Jackson: "Your best friend showed me the way to the mountain where the spirits lit up the night."

Taciana: "You mean it is actually true?"

Jackson: "Yes."

Taciana: "That is incredible, Jacky! I seriously like the new you."

Jackson: "You mean you are not freaked out by my appearance?"

Taciana: "No, of course not. I like you for who you are and not just for your dashing appearance."

Jackson: "Wow, thanks. You really are one of a kind, Taciana Rabeau."

Taciana: "What kind of furry are you anyways?"

Jackson: "I am a dashing dhole, baby."

Taciana: "So you are an attractive canine, huh?"

Ramona: "This is unbelievable. Those two could wake up a city! They are so loud! I should be the one in there with him. Not her!"

Ramona walks to Taciana's room and slowly creaks the door open, revealing her sister and Jackson, now a furry, looking at a computer. She closes the door and knocks on it loudly. Taciana tries to ignore her sister but realizes that Ramona will never cease until she has gotten what she wanted.

Jackson: "Should we ignore her?"

Taciana: "No, Jacky. We cannot just ignore her. I will take care of it. Ramona, I am coming! Sheesh! What is it?"

Mrs. Rabeau: "Girls! There is no yelling allowed in this household. You two need to learn about getting along."

Ramona: "But Momma, she won't share Jackson with me."

Taciana: "My Jacky is not a toy. He's a living individual who deserves only one love in his life."

Ramona: "Huh, and you think that is you? Dream on, sister!"

Taciana: "Well yeah. I am the one who saved him."

Ramona: "Serena, Tawny, and I saw him too."

Taciana: "Oh please, you three are just out to take him away for yourselves. I have actually been getting to know the real him during lunch time at school."

Ramona: "Hmph, we will see who gets him one day, sister! You'll see!"

Warrick: "Hey, could you keep it down, Ramona?"

Ramona: "No! I'm in my room. Alone."

Warrick: "Ramona? Are you okay? I hear you sniffling."

Ramona: "Just go away."

Warrick: "Look, you won't get Jackson at all with the way you're acting. And I'm pretty sure he's picked Taciana."

Ramona: "But I love him so much!"

Warrick: "Sis, you could find someone else."

Ramona: "I don't want someone else. I want Jackson!"

Warrick: "Not gonna happen, sis. Look, I'll see you later, okay? Renet's waiting for me."

.......3 hours later.......

Woman: "Welcome child. How may I be of service?"

Ramona: "Good afternoon. Ms. Velder, right?"

Woman: "Velderman."

Ramona: "Got it. I am here to see who I am destined to be with."

Dorian Velderman: "Hold out the palm of your paw and touch the sacred orb."

Ramona: "Okay."

Dorian: "Ooooom."

Ramona: "Is there anything?"

Dorian: "Shush. Have patience, child. Your special someone is a furry unlike any other."

Ramona: "Really?"

Dorian: "Yes. He is strong and highly intelligent."

Ramona: "Yay! What genus of furry is he?"

Dorian: "He is of the canine genus."

Ramona: "Yes! I knew it!"

Dorian: "However, unless you can change his mind, he will never acknowledge your feelings. That is all the orb can show."

Ramona: "Is this session free?"

Dorian: "Nope."

Ramona: "How much?"

Dorian: "Five dollars."

Ramona: "Oh okay. Thank you for the insight, Ms. Velderman."

Dorian: "Anytime."

Ramona: "Now I know exactly what to do to win my Jackson's heart."

Back to School

The Next Day.

Jackson: "Are you set for today, Tacci?"

Taciana: "I have been ready for Monday since last Friday. Today we get to find out what we need to do for our Flats for Furries project!"

Jackson: "I am grateful that you and your family accepted me as one of your own."

Jackson starts up his new car and Taciana hops in on the passenger side.

Jackson: "Where is Warrick?"

Taciana: "He left early to go pick up Renet."

Jackson: "Should we wait for your sisters or just leave them to walk it out?"

Taciana: "We could leave them, but then they would probably hate us for the rest of the day."

Jackson: "Alright, we will wait."

Then after ten minutes of waiting, the rest of the Rabeau sisters jump in the back and the five zoom off to school.

Jackson: "Alright, here we are, ladies. Wait, Taciana, I'll get your door."

Taciana: "Such a gentleman."

Jackson: "My pleasure, sweet Tacia."

Natasha: "Are you prepared for the biology quiz today, Carina?"

Carina: "I have been prepared since a couple of days ago."

Natasha: "You actually prepared for a quiz?"

Carina: "Yes, I am actually ready for it."

Natasha: "Why are you smiling so much?"

Carina: "No reason."

Natasha: "You met someone you like, didn't you?"

Carina: "I had some help studying from someone special."

Natasha: "Awww. What is his name?"

Carina: "His name is Jackson Tontione."

Natasha: "You mean the human?"

Carina: "He is a furry now."

Natasha: "What species of furry is he?"

Carina: "He is a very strong and intelligent dhole."

Natasha: "Woah, is that him with the Rabeaus?"

Carina: "Yeah."

Natasha: "Well, he certainly is a handsome one."

Carina: "He's coming this way."

Jackson: "Hey girl. How is it going?"

Carina: "Hi, Jackson."

Jackson: "Who is your friend?"

Carina: "This is Natasha Rouille and we were about to head to class, but could we walk with you and the Rabeaus?"

Jackson: "Yes, of course you can."

Carina: "Yay! Thank you."

Taciana: "Paws off Carina, he is my mate."

Carina: "Sorry bestie, he is just too handsome to resist."

Jackson: "Well, we should be getting to the gym for the assembly. See you there!"

Taciana: "Wait for me, Jacky!"

.......Three minutes later.......

Principal: "Students, thank you all for coming. This week we have a special project for you. On Thursday and Friday you will all be helping to build Flats for Furries!"

Students: "Yay!"

Principal: "These homes will help those among us who are less fortunate. Even if you have never helped build a home before, there is a job for you. We need furries to carry things, paint, rake the yard, and deliver things. Everyone can help."

Students: "Hooray! We can all help!"

Jackson: "Taciana, are you sure this will be fun?"

Serena: "You bet, Jackson! Helping others is always fun. I always paint."

Tawny: "And I always help decorate."

Ramona: "I help install the windows."

Taciana: "And I like to help put down carpet. It's not hard at all, you'll see. Everyone pitching in together makes it go quickly!"

Jackson: "Well, if you four ladies can do all that, I bet I can do something too."

Principal: "…and that's when we will meet. Time for class now, everyone."

…….6 hours and 48 minutes later…….

Carina: "Glad that's over."

Natasha: "Thank goodness."

Taciana: "You said it."

Jackson: "You all want to go to the skating rink at the arcade?"

Warrick: "I'm down."

Renet: "Sounds fun!"

Jackson: "Awesome! Let's roll."

Taciana, Carina, and Natasha jump in Jackson's car. Warrick and Renet follow in the truck. The other three Rabeau sisters took the bus after realizing they were left behind.

Skating

As the three sisters head towards home, Riley and her friends call out to them.

Riley: "Hey Ramona!"

Ramona: "Oh hi, Riley."

Riley: "Are you three going roller skating?"

Ramona: "We sure are. Are you all going too?"

Riley: "Absolutely. Say, do you want to hitch a ride with us and see if we can still make it there on time?"

Ramona: "We are in."

Riley: "Alright ladies, time to go rock and roll—on skates! Hey Evelyn, who are you texting?"

Evelyn: "Oh, I'm just texting my boyfriend Yahar about where to meet at the rink."

Abby: "Oooh, someone wants to have fun tonight, huh?"

Evelyn: "Stop, it's just roller skating."

Evelyn: "What about you Abby?"

Abby: "I want to have a good time dancing, obviously. I guess you three probably wanted to go because Jackson is going to be there. Am I right?"

Ramona: "What is he to you?"

Abby: "I know he is strong and clever and not only that but Riley cannot get her mind off of him."

Tawny: "He belongs to Taciana, Riley. But I bet we can find you a date."

.......Forty Minutes Later.......

Riley: "Okay, here we are! The Owl Roller Rink."

Ramona: "Cool. We will be seeing you three later. Come on, sisters."

Riley: "See ya then."

Evelyn: "I'll catch you girls later, my Yahar waits for me."

Yahar: "Hey there, my clawed lady. What is shaking?"

Evelyn: "Oh, nothing, you kidder, I just came here with my friends so we can go roller skating."

Yahar: "Well, it just so happens that I have my custom skates on right now."

Evelyn: "Those look cool on you, Yahar."

Yahar: "Why thank you, milady. I could rent you out some skates if you want to join me in a dance."

Evelyn: "Yeah, I would love to dance with you."

Yahar: "I'll be right back, my rough forest rose."

Evelyn: "Okay! I'll–wow that was fast! You are back so quickly, my handsome honey badger."

Yahar: "It is all about power of persuasion, plus a rental discount."

Evelyn: "Awesome!"

Yahar: "Shall we?"

Taciana: "Jackson?"

Jackson: "Huh?"

Taciana: "I was asking if you want to take me for a spin on the skating rink."

Jackson: "Sure, Tacci."

Natasha: "I'd like to dance too."

Carina: "Actually I am dancing with him first."

Taciana: "No I am."

Natasha: "Me first!"

Jackson: "Ladies please, I will dance with all of you."

Taciana: "I am willing to share him with the rest of you."

Carina: "I thought you weren't big on sharing."

Taciana: "I'm only sharing him for tonight, bestie."

Carina: "Can we just dance, please?"

Natasha: "Yeah."

Jackson: "There is a good song playing, ladies. Let's party."

.......An hour later.......

Ramona: "No one will skate with me!"

Serena: "Me either."

Tawny: "Or me."

Serena: "Let's just go home."

.......Meanwhile ....

Riley walks out on the rink and skates in Jackson's direction. One of her old friends, Tobias the Chipmunk, approaches her after seeing her alone.

Tobias: "Hey Riley."

Riley: "Oh, hi Tobias."

Tobias: "I was wondering if you would care to dance."

Riley: "Tobias, you and I are friends, right? But I have my eye on someone else."

Tobias: "Who?"

Riley: "Him. Jackson. He's skating with everyone else and is really good, so I want to skate with him too."

Tobias: "He doesn't look that special."

Abby: "I'll dance with you, Tobias."

Tobias: "Didn't expect that from you, Abby."

Abby: "Why not, Toby Reyes? I am a very saucy squirrel, baby. Let's dance."

Riley then skates onto the floor herself, only to bump into Kendall instead.

Kendall: "Watch it, Riley!"

Riley: "Sorry, Kendall."

Kendall: "How about you make it up to me, huh?"

Riley: "What? No."

Kendall: "Come on, I know we broke up, but I miss skating with you."

Riley: "Let go of me!"

Kendall: "You remember when you said I was your weasel?"

Riley: "That was five years ago and I'm over you. Bye."

Kendall starts to get angry but Jackson sees what's happening and shoves Kendall backwards against the column.

Jackson: "She said lay off, weasel."

Kendall: "This does not concern you."

Jackson: "If I see something wrong, then I make it my business. Riley, you alright?"

Riley: "Yeah. Thanks for saving me."

Jackson: "Not a problem."

Riley: "Where did your friends go?"

Jackson: "Carina got a little motion sickness and Taciana and the others left for home."

Riley: "You mean you lent them your ride?"

Jackson: "Only Taciana can drive my ride, besides me. Hey, your cheek is bleeding. Here is an antiseptic wipe to put on it."

Riley: "I don't think I can drive home while holding this on my cheek."

Jackson: "No worries Riley, I can drive you home."

Riley: "Are you always this sweet to girls you rescue?"

Jackson: "Depends on the girl, but we are good friends, so of course."

Skating Part II

Jackson: "You want to sit up front or the back?"

Riley: "The back seat works. I have a question?"

Jackson: "Ask away."

Riley: "Why did you save me?"

Jackson: "I protected you because I care about what happens to others and will right the wrongs caused by those who do harm."

Riley: "Wow. That is very wise and noble of you."

Jackson: "I tried that all the time back when I was a human, but it did not make much of a difference in that world. Here, it is vastly different. The world I see now is a lot greener than it was before and filled with many possibilities."

Riley: "Your smarts are really impressing me now, Jackson Tontione."

Jackson: "Thanks, Riley."

Jackson drives Riley home and helps her inside of the house.

Riley: "I really had fun skating even if I could not be with you while being there."

Jackson: "Riley, I would have invited you to come along with us if you had just asked me."

Riley: "Really?"

Jackson: "Yeah, of course I would."

Riley: "Thanks, Jackson! Maybe we can work together when we build the house."

Jackson: "That's a great idea, Riley. We can all make a difference when we work together. We can have fun doing it too!"

Jackson vs Bruno: Fight for Life

Jackson wakes up and heads into the main house's kitchen for breakfast. As he walked, he thought about how kind everyone had been to him so far. He wondered why when he was a human living on Earth, he had never seen people so happy all the time. Here, there were a few bullies, but for the most part, everyone worked to get along.

Jackson: "Mmmm. What is that delectable smell?"

Taciana: "Hello, Jackson."

Jackson: "Tacci! You're up early."

Taciana: "Of course I am up early. I made your favorite. Mixed berry pancakes!"

Jackson: "You are an awesome cook."

Taciana: "Thanks, baby."

.......Twenty Minutes Later.......

Jackson: "Very satisfying. Burrrrp! Pardon me."

Taciana: "Consider yourself excused, darling."

Jackson: "What is it, my ravishing bunny? You are staring at me."

Taciana: "Oh nothing, it is just you are being you. Also, I happen to have one more pancake left on the center plate, sugar."

Jackson: "You want to share it? I can cut it in half for you."

Taciana: "Mmmm. It was so tasty. Now, let's go my handsome dhole, we have to get ready for school today."

Jackson: "We've still got an hour."

Taciana: "It's better to be early."

Ms. Rabeau: "Shouldn't you two be getting to school now?"

Taciana: "We will, Momma. Come on Jacky, it is your turn to drive."

She tosses him his keys as she places her backpack in the back seat.

Taciana: "Where were you last night? I didn't see you before bedtime."

Jackson: "I was helping Riley."

Taciana: "The girl from the dealership?"

Jackson: "Yeah."

Taciana: "With what?"

Jackson: "I was tending her wounds from last night on the rink."

Taciana: "How was she hurt?"

Jackson: "Some weasel wearing brown gloves slashed her face out of rage and I warned him to back off."

Taciana: "Oh, you mean Kendall?"

Jackson: "Yeah, him."

Taciana: "He used to date Riley back in middle school until he tried forcing her to steal the valuables of others."

Jackson: "Really? Did she go along with it?"

Taciana: "No, and I am glad she refused to help him."

Taciana: "I know you two are friends, but don't let her get too friendly with you, okay?"

Jackson: "Tacci, it is fine. Nothing happened between me and her."

Taciana: "Good."

.......Ten minutes Later.......

Jackson and Taciana arrive at school and see Warrick, Renet, Carina, Natasha, Abby, Tobias, Evelyn, Yahar, and Riley at the school's entrance, just hanging out and waiting for the front doors to open.

Riley: "There he is! I was so glad he helped me last night."

Abby: "Me too. But isn't it sweet how Taciana is the one he loves because he felt a strong connection with her the moment he saw her?"

Tobias: "I didn't know you were the type to know about interpersonal emotions."

Abby: "I can be romantic Toby, I just wanted to wait for the right time to tell you."

Natasha: "Shhh, they are coming this way!"

Taciana: "Morning, everyone!"

Warrick: "Looks like we beat you two here, sis."

Taciana: "Where are our sisters?"

Renet: "Warrick told me that they are still sleeping in and might come in late again."

Warrick: "They often are."

Renet: "Warrick, they are your sisters and you can't just leave them behind for your convenience every day."

Warrick: "I know sweet cheeks, but they have been annoying ever since early childhood. They argue all the time. For no reason."

Renet: "Just try to be there for them too, okay."

Warrick: "Fine, alright already! I promise."

Renet: "Thanks, sweetie."

Warrick: "However, for the next few rides it's only going to be us, deal?"

Jackson: "School doors are open, let's go in everybody."

Carina: "Yeah, time to keep our GPAs above the four-point zero range."

Jackson: "Something wrong, Carina?"

Carina: "I am really not a morning type of gal."

Jackson: "Okay then."

.......Five hours Later.......

It's lunch time and everyone is sitting at the middle table. The room is noisy with students talking and laughing. Everyone is enjoying their lunch break until Bruno and his crew cause a ruckus just outside the lunchroom.

Bruno: "Listen ladies, either you all come with us to prom this spring or we make you."

Sophia: "We are not going with you jerks after what you've all become. I'm out of here."

Bruno: "I didn't say you could walk away yet, you cheating witch."

Sophia: "Let go of me! Stop it!"

Bruno: "Cyprus, grab the wolverine girl."

Cyprus: "Already got her restrained, bro."

Gulani the Wolverine: "Get your mitts off me!"

Cyprus: "Quiet girl."

Gulani: "You are crazy!"

Louie: "Stop squirming, Pepper!"

Pepper the Grey Fox: "You three are awful examples of responsible students!"

Louie: "You think we care about that? Just keep your mouth silent."

Pepper: "You should care! Somebody help us, please!"

.......Meanwhile in the Lunch Room.......

Jackson: "Taciana?"

Taciana: "Yes, Jacky?"

Jackson: "Is anyone going to help them out there?"

Taciana: "There's usually a security guard patrolling the halls but I have not seen any of them today."

Jackson: "Is he off for the day?"

Taciana: "I'm not sure. Don't be a hero, Jackson. I don't want to see you hurt."

Jackson: "I know, Tacci, but someone has to intervene and stop the madness."

He squeezes Taciana's hand then walks outside the lunchroom, seeing the three bullies holding Sophia and the two other furry girls against their will.

Taciana: "Be careful."

Jackson: "Hey! Beast One to Three! You all like harassing innocent furry girls, huh?"

Bruno: "Keep walking, dhole!"

Cyprus: "Yeah get moving!"

Louie: "This matter doesn't concern you, dawg."

Jackson: "Actually fools, that is where you are all mistaken. Now let these three beautiful ladies go."

Bruno: "Who do you think you are?"

Jackson: "I was the guy you attacked before. Now it is time someone taught you a lesson about how to treat a lady."

Cyprus: "I got this one. Let me at him!"

Cyprus charges Jackson, roaring. Jackson ducks and trips Cyprus, making him land flat on the ground, groaning in pain. Jackson looks at the other two bullies.

Jackson: "Who's next?"

Bruno: "You got some grit on you. How about a little wager, Tontione?"

Jackson: "Name it."

Bruno: "If me and my crew win, you can't mess with our business."

Jackson: "Deal. However, if I win, these three ladies go free and you won't mess anyone else at school ever again."

Louie: "That is crazy Bruno. I ain't going for that."

Bruno: "We accept your challenge, Tontione. This will all go down outside at the abandoned scrapyard after school."

Jackson: "Fine, but until you win, you cannot bother Sophia or the other two ladies here."

Cyprus: "We will be ready, dhole. Just have an emergency room ready after we clobber you."

The three bullies walk away to the courtyard behind the school to prepare for the fight. Jackson turns back to the three girls.

Sophia: "That was awesome!"

Jackson: "No problem, Sophie."

Sophia: "You are my strong hero."

Jackson: "Who are your friends?"

Sophia: "This is Gulani, and this is Pepper."

Jackson: "Nice to officially meet you two, even under that turn of events."

Gulani and Pepper just giggle at him; Taciana has been watching and instantly crushes a lemon in jealousy.

Warrick: "Chill, sis, he is not leaving you for another girl."

Taciana: "I know Warrick, I am just concerned that he is letting his newfound strength and popularity get to his head."

Warrick: "Tacci, he writes poems about you when you are not around. I think your position as his girlfriend is set in stone."

Taciana: "Thanks, big brother. Just keep my bestie happy, alright?"

Warrick: "I am keeping her away from the fight, but she still wants to watch it anyways."

Taciana walks out to greet the crowd in the hallway with a strut and pulls Jackson into a deep smooch on the mouth to make a point.

Taciana: "Hi girls and Sophia. Glad you two met my boyfriend, Jackson Tontione."

Jackson: "I forgot to mention to you that Taciana Rabeau is my girl."

Pepper: "You will save us from those brutish knuckleheads, right Jackson?"

Jackson: "You bet your bright brown eyes I will. Those fools will never win. Now, it is time to prepare for my victory."

Jackson vs Bruno: Winning the Heart

Jackson invites Sophia and her friends to the lunchroom table with the others he had been sitting with. They all crowd around the table.

Taciana: "I am worried this might not end well. What if you cannot win this?"

Jackson: "Hey, hey, I will always survive regardless and come back to you, okay?"

Taciana: "Okay."

Taciana scoots closer to him and lays her head against his shoulder for comfort.

Sophia: "Jackson?"

Jackson: "What's up, Sophie?"

Sophia: "Could we talk outside in private for a moment?"

Jackson: "Be right back, Tacci."

.......Outside in the hallway.......

Jackson: "You wanted to ask me something?"

Sophia: "I've been wanting to give you this. Mmwah."

Jackson: "What was that kiss for?"

Sophia: "It is my way of saying thanks for coming to help me and my friends. I was so frightened by what they might have done if you hadn't shown up."

Jackson: "It's okay, that meat head is not gonna lay a paw on you after today. Hey, so how is little Tia doing?"

Sophia: "She is alright, but she says she misses you."

Jackson: "Am I a better storyteller than you?"

Sophia: "Yes, and she wants you to come over again for a visit."

Jackson: "I'll stop by sometime, sure."

.......Three hours later.......

The school bell rings to signal the finish of the school day. Everyone in the school has either left on the buses or driven home. Jackson and his friends reach the scrapyard early and wait for Bruno and his crew to arrive.

Warrick: "Here we are, everyone. The scrapyard."

Jackson: "Kinda reminds me of the junkyards from the old world."

Taciana: "Jackson, this isn't exactly a safe place to face off against those three."

Jackson: "Trust me I got this."

Taciana: "Be careful."

Jackson walks to the center of the scrapyard and stands at the ready. A large pickup truck rolls in.

Bruno: "Guess you were serious about this after all. I was starting to think you would be a no show since I am going to enjoy having Sophia as my own when I win."

Jackson: "Enough talk! Let's just finish this."

Bruno: "Very well."

Bruno runs at Jackson to take the first swing but misses. Jackson ducks and strikes back at Bruno's stomach and evades another blow from Cyprus.

Cyprus: "You are gonna...Whoa!"

Cyprus is tripped by Jackson's quick reflexes. Louie rushes in and tackles Jackson to the ground with ease. Jackson growls and kicks him hard in the shin.

Louie: "Owwww!"

Bruno: "You're gonna pay for roughing up my crew!"

Jackson: "Do you really want to try attacking me again?"

Bruno: "Raaaah!"

Jackson: "Too slow Bruno."

Bruno: "What! How?"

Jackson: "Three words Bruno; intense exercise regimen. Looks like I won."

Bruno tries to strike him while his back is turned, but is stopped by Warrick who steps in.

Warrick: "This is how you act when you have lost? Shameful. Even if he is not from this world, my bro Jackson has much more dignity than you."

Bruno: "Fine, you have freed the girls, but don't think this war is over, Jack. We will beat you someday."

Jackson: "Yeah, good luck with that."

As Bruno and his cohorts leave the scrapyard in Cyprus' hybrid truck, the whole gang comes down to congratulate Jackson's victory, cheering him with excitement. The girls cluster around Jackson, hugging and kissing him.

Sophia: "Jackson! I don't even know what to say."

Gulani: "Yeah."

Pepper: "We cannot thank you enough for protecting us from that awful Bruno and his followers."

Jackson: "Ladies, take it easy now."

Renet: "Aren't you going to say something about all that, Taciana?"

Taciana: "I know for a fact that my Jackson would never hurt me. Besides, I'm going to go join in."

Jackson: "Tacci, I did it! I won the match!"

Taciana: "I saw. Make way you three, the main girl is coming through. It's my turn for a victory kiss."

Renet: "Warrick?"

Warrick: "Yeah, bae?"

Renet: "That was so righteous of you to help Jackson down there. Especially right after that brawl was officially over."

Warrick: "The right thing is its own reward, Renet."

Renet: "That is not the only reward."

Abby: "Tobias, could we also have some alone time?"

Tobias: "Yeah, but probably over the weekend since we have to stay focused."

Abby: "Toby, all of us here might be seniors but that doesn't mean we don't deserve a little down time."

Evelyn: "You two make a good couple."

Yahar: "They are not the only ones who make a good pair."

Evelyn: "Friday night is our first official date night, Yahar."

Yahar: "I remember, my delightful sweet pie."

Evelyn: "You are so silly."

Build Day!

When the night reaches its end and is greeted by a miraculously perfect morning, Jackson Tontione stirs as the light from the open window blinds shines over him.

Jackson: "Ooh, yeah. Another day, another subject to learn about in the world. Wait! Today is the day we start to build the houses! I better find some work clothes."

Warrick: "Jackson! Are you awake? I'm heading to the school with the girls. Jump in! Time to go!"

Jackson: "Hang on! I'm almost ready."

Jackson quickly gets into the truck, wearing his work clothes. Taciana and her sisters are grinning at him and chattering excitedly, also dressed in work clothes. The teenagers pick up breakfast on the way and dash towards school. None of them can wait to get started. Their friends are all waiting as they drive up to the high school parking lot and rush over. The teachers are outside and there are several buses filled with teenage furries.

Principal: "Listen up! Today we are going to be building Flats for Furries! You will all be split into groups when we get to the build site. Pay attention to the teacher in charge, they will assign your jobs. Also, be careful! We don't want anyone hurt."

Quickly Jackson and the others climb on board one of the busses.

Serena: "I am so excited! This will be great. Missing school and helping others!"

Warrick: "It's a good thing I'm here. They'll need my muscles to help."

Jackson: "I wonder what job I will be assigned."

A teacher walks down the bus as it drives slowly through the town. She hands each person a slip of paper with their name on it, and their job.

Jackson: "Huh. Installing windows."

Taciana: "Me too! We will be working together!"

Tawny: "Ohh there it is! Just ahead!"

The busses pull in and the friends separate by groups. Jackson is glad to be with several people he already knows. For the rest of the day, the furry teenagers work hard. They build the frame for the house, then put up the sides, all working together. Some furries hang the doors while others, like Taciana and Jackson, put in windows. It's getting late, but the house Jackson is working on is nearly done.

Ramona: "Whew. I'm tired. Tomorrow when we come back, we get to do the really fun stuff!"

Serena: "Yeah! Painting and decorating, and fixing up the outside!"

Jackson: "I have to admit, this is a lot more fun than I thought it would be. It was pretty amazing getting to be part of this."

Taciana: "It's not over yet, my handsome dhole. Just wait til it's completed. I bet you feel even prouder. I know I'm so proud of you for helping! Tonight, we should go have dinner out. I want to take you to my favorite place. It's really yummy, you'll love it. And we deserve the treat for working so hard."

Jackson: "Whatever you say, honey bunny. But I think I need to get cleaned up first! I've been working hard, and smell like it, too."

Taciana: "Oh Jackson! You are so funny! Yes, let's go home and get ready."

Everyone climbs back onto the busses. As they drive away, Jackson can't help but think how amazing it was that just a few hours ago, there was a grassy bit of land, now, there's an almost finished house.

Jackson: "So where should we go for dinner?"

Taciana: "Oh, we have to go to this one restaurant known as the Golden Aqua, babe!"

Jackson: "You got a deal, bunny bunch."

Dinner

Jackson starts the engine and hits the automatic door button for Taciana.

Jackson: "Hop in."

Taciana: "I didn't know you had an automatic door option for this car."

Jackson: "This ride is full of surprises, bunny boo."

Taciana: "Oh you."

.......At the Restaurant.......

A young raccoon waitress named Ava comes up to them and seats them at an outdoor table. It's a quiet atmosphere, perfect for a private dinner.

Ava: "Hi there, folks, I am Ava and I will be taking care of you for the night."

Jackson: "Hello, Ava. I would like the grand feast with the garlic shrimp, lobster tail, crab legs, mussels, and a side salad."

Ava: "Okay. What would you like to drink, hun?"

Jackson: "She and I will have two mango daiquiris without the rum."

Ava: "Got all of that. What would you like to have, miss?"

Taciana: "I will take a full vegetable platter with a side of garlic bread."

Ava: "Coming right up."

.......Two minutes later.......

Ava: "Hey Vern! I need one full veggie platter, one grand feast with a salad, and two mango daiquiris with no rum!"

Vern: "Sure thing, Ava. I am on it!"

.......Fifty minutes later.......

Vern: "Order up, Ava!!!"

Ava: "Thanks Vern."

Ava carries the heavy tray outside and gasps at the sight before her. Jackson and Taciana are holding hands and dancing to the music of the small band outside near their table.

Ava: "Ahem. Hi there, your food is ready. Here you go."

Jackson: "Oh right. Babe, our food awaits."

Taciana: "Excellent."

Jackson: "This all looks delicious. Thank you."

Ava: "You're welcome."

Taciana: "Why did she only say that to you, but not me?"

Jackson: "Sweetheart, don't think about that and let's enjoy our dinner, okay?"

Taciana: "Alright."

.......1 hour and 30 minutes later.......

Taciana: "I am so full, bae. Could we save the rest for later when we return home?"

Jackson: "Definitely, Tacci. Also, I would rather save the food for tomorrow's dinner than to waste it."

Taciana: "Glad you agree, honey. Ava!"

Ava: "Yes?"

Taciana: "Could we get some carry out boxes to take home, please?"

Ava: "Absolutely! Be right back."

Jackson: "See no need for suspicion."

Taciana: "You are right, I was worried for nothing."

.......Five minutes Later.......

Ava gave them three take home boxes for their leftovers and placed the receipt in the center of the table showing how much they owe.

Taciana: "This whole meal costs one hundred and fifty dollars."

Jackson: "We can split the check, Tacci, no worries. You can pay seventy-five and I'll pay seventy-five."

Taciana: "My intelligent boyfriend. Sounds good to me."

She places her and Jackson's debit cards on the table.

Jackson: "Thanks for getting your mom to find a way for me to make payments."

Taciana: "It's no biggie baby. I am simply happy that I got to spend this night with you."

Ava: "Okay, you're all set. Have a wonderful night, folks."

Jackson: "Bye, Ava."

Taciana: "Bye."

Ava then starts cleaning the table and notices a fifty-dollar cash tip left with a note.

Writing on the Note: "You showed exceptional customer service Ava. Here is your gratuity."

Ava: "He left this for me? The buff and handsome dhole furry left this for me!"

Shauna: "Someone looks happy."

Ava: "Just that this is the best shift of my life."

Shauna: "Huh, right."

.......35 Minutes Later.......

Jackson and Taciana arrive back home to a worried Mrs. and Mr. Rabeau at the front door with their feet tapping.

Mrs. Rabeau: "Where have you two been? It is past eleven o'clock at night."

Mr. Rabeau: "Go upstairs and get some sleep immediately, Taciana!"

Taciana: "Daddy, we were just out having dinner."

Jackson: "She is right, sir. Nothing bad happened."

Mr. Rabeau: "Hmmm, alright then."

Taciana: "We better get to bed, Jackson! We've got to finish our school project tomorrow, building the homes."

Jackson: "You are right. I can't wait to finish. Goodnight everyone!"

Vandalism!

The next morning Jackson joins Taciana and her sisters and brother for a quick breakfast of fruit and yogurt, then they hurry to the school. They pull up and climb onto one of the busses filled with excited furries talking about how great it will be to finish the homes today for the furries who will be moving in. Several of the students are holding plants and flowers to put into the yard. As the bus Jackson and his team is on arrives at the house they'd worked so hard on the day before, silence fills the air.

Serena: "What… what happened?"

Ramona: "Our house! It's… ruined!"

Tawny: "Who could have done such a thing?"

Jackson and the others slowly climbed off the bus. The house, which was nearly complete the day before, was now a disaster. The windows were all broken. The doors were torn off. Someone had put big holes into the wall. Even the grass had been damaged by large tire tracks crossing all over the yard. All of their hard work was now ruined.

Taciana: "This is a disaster. Who could be so mean?"

Jackson: "I don't know. But there's only one thing we can do."

The other students crowded around him and listened.

Jackson: "No matter how bad it is, we've got to fix it. Furries are relying on us. Come on guys, we can do it!"

Taciana: "Jackson is right! Come on everyone! No stopping til it is perfect!"

Everyone: "Hooray for Jackson! Let's get it fixed!"

Together the teenage furries spend the rest of the day fixing up the house. They replace the windows and they patch the holes in the walls. Together they rehang the doors, and several of the teenagers rake the yard and spread down grass seed in the damaged parts. They worked until the sun was about to set and all of them were nearly collapsing with exhaustion.

Taciana: "I'm so tired, even my fur hurts."

Jackson: "But we got it done. It's all ready for that furry family to move in tomorrow."

Taciana: "It looks so much better now. Even the garden looks nice with the flowers planted."

Ramona: "We couldn't have done it without you, Jackson."

Serena: "Yeah. Thank you for inspiring us!"

Jackson: "It's important to help others. When things get tough, it's important to keep going and not give up."

Tawny: "You are so inspiring, Jackson!"

Taciana: "That's my dhole! I'm so proud of you, bae. Now let's go. I can't wait to get dinner and get some sleep. I can hardly keep my eyes open."

Ramona: "I'm tired, too."

Serena: "I'm more tired than you!"

Tawny: "Humph. I'm the most tired of everyone!"

Birthday Prep

Jackson stirs at the sound of someone knocking on the guest cottage door. Sleepily, he stumbles and sees Taciana. She is already dressed and hops in cheerfully.

Jackson: "Tacci, it is only five thirty in the morning. Chill."

Taciana: "Sweetie, the earlier we wake up the better. We're going shopping for gifts and party supplies before Serena's birthday next week."

Jackson: "Mmmm. I am not much of a shopping fan."

Taciana: "Come on, baby. Do it for me. And for Serena. Please?"

Jackson: "What would your sister enjoy as a gift?"

Taciana: "Well, I know she's been dying to receive this special mango perfume. Come on, lover boy, let's find a gift for Serena so we can enjoy some mini golf at the park later."

Jackson: "I look forward to it. I can't wait to try that hole with the windmill."

Taciana and Jackson head to a large store. After several minutes of searching for Serena's gift, they notice Mr. and Mrs. Rabeau are also collecting and purchasing party supplies.

Jackson: "Your parents are here shopping for the party supplies so I guess that means we can simply purchase this birthday card and the mango scented perfume and roll out."

Taciana: "Hmmm, okay."

They head to the checkout register and purchase the items from the clerk. Quickly they leave and drive back to the Rabeau household.

Taciana: "Here we are."

Jackson: "Now that we're back with Serena's gifts I also bought a little something for you when your back was turned."

Taciana: "Jackson, you didn't have to do that."

Jackson: "I wanted to do it anyway, because you are the beautiful and outstanding bunny girl who rescued me from that stasis pod."

Taciana: "Oh my gosh! What a beautiful necklace! It looks divine, sweetie."

Jackson: "Look on the pendant."

Taciana: "You engraved my initials into it?"

Jackson: "Of course, Tacci. Care for a dance, bunny girl?"

Taciana: "Stereo, play a smooth R&B soul song."

Electronic Device: "Yes, confirmed. Playing now."

Taciana: "You are a terrific dancer."

Jackson: "So are you."

They stayed that way for hours, like nobody was around to interrupt this very tender moment.

The Party

.......One Week Later.......

Serena walks inside from picking up some berries in the garden after a long school day and finds the whole house seemingly deserted.

Serena: "Hello? Anyone? What's this? Arrows on the ground. Huh? They lead into the family ballroom."

Everyone: "Surprise!"

Serena: "Thank you! All my friends and family came out to celebrate my eighteenth birthday!"

Jackson: "We even bought a DJ to play any song you desire."

Serena: "This is so awesome Jackson! Thank you! Thank you!"

Jackson: "Shouldn't you be having fun or go play some party games?"

Serena: "Oh, but I already am having fun."

Taciana: "Hey, paws off birthday girl."

Serena: "It is my birthday, which means I get whatever and whoever I want."

Taciana: "Listen here, sister. You're going to regret messing with my man!"

Jackson: "Tacci, just stop please. I am not going leave you for Serena. It's your sister's birthday and I don't want any conflict between any of us."

Serena: "DJ! Turn up the music!"

DJ Ovossy: "Yeah! You got it."

The music starts up and booms all around. The crowd dances freestyle. Everyone is having a great time.

Abby: "This is so much fun, Toby!"

Tobias: "Oh, I know."

Abby: "Go baby! Shake it!"

Warrick and Renet are dancing "The Robot" together.

Warrick: "I'm the robotic dancing master!"

Renet: "I beg to differ! Check out this move!"

Warrick: "Totally unfair, Renet."

Renet: "I'm in the lead for the dance contest winner, handsome!"

.......Meanwhile ....

Riley dances in a graceful circle when the song changes from a fast pace to a slow and a suave melody emerging from the music amplifiers.

Male Ferret Furry: "Hey there, Riley."

Riley: "Who are you?"

Male Ferret Furry: "You are kidding right? It's me Miles."

Riley: "Oh right, from last year's chemistry class. Are you enjoying yourself?"

Miles: "Yeah, I have never been invited to the Rabeau's house before."

Riley: "Hehehe. It is almost like a mansion, except it has one guest room."

Miles: "You ought to join me and my friends by the amplifiers. The music sounds better if you're really close to them."

Riley follows her new acquaintance. They both feel the graceful intensity of the music, along with everyone else on the dance floor.

Evelyn: "Huh, well what do you know. It looks like Riley finally has made a new friend. I'm happy for her."

Yahar: "I told you she'd be fine, Eve. Let's dance."

Evelyn: "You are good for someone who likes to keep me on my feet."

Yahar: "My aim is too please, Badgera."

.......One Hour Later.......

Ramona is sitting alone in her room. She draws in her diary while listening to the party downstairs.

Ramona: "This music sounds off the chain, but it would be so much better if I had someone to dance with. Since I don't, I'm just going to stay here until someone gets me."

Tawny: "Ramona? Come on, sis! It's nearly time for Serena to blow out her candles."

Ramona: "Alright! I'm coming."

Tawny: "Mom and Dad couldn't stay because they have a late night board meeting with their company investors."

Ramona: "They are always busy on weekends, Tawny. What's the point?"

Tawny: "The point is being there for Serena because she's growing up just like us. Plus, we're her family and we should celebrate the day of her birth like we always do."

Ramona: "Fine, Serena can have her day, but later on it will be my chance."

Tawny: "Whatever you say, Ramona."

Jackson: "Taciana?"

Taciana: "Yes, babe?"

Jackson: "I think Serena is getting antsy to make her birthday wish. She whispered in my ear she wanted to have some cake as she walked off the dance floor."

Taciana: "Okay. I'll grab the megaphone. Ahem. Is this working? Attention everyone! It is time to wish my baby sister a great happy birthday!"

Serena's Wish

Serena: "Finally, I can make my wish as an eighteen-year-old."

Everyone: "Happy Birthday to you!"

Serena: "Thank you everyone. This is a dream come true."

She blows out all the candles on the chocolate fudge cake with carrots on top. The crowd cheers out with a loud applause after she finishes blowing the eighteenth candle.

Ramona: "Congrats, Serena."

Tawny: "Yeah, congrats."

Ramona: "Nice pipes, Jackson. I didn't know you could sing like that."

Jackson: "Thanks, Ramona. However, Taciana was my co-star."

Taciana: "Let's hear your birthday wish, sister!"

Serena: "I wish to have the best birthday ever! Let's dance, everyone!"

The teenagers keep dancing and spend the rest of the night eating cake and watching Serena open her presents. She's excited that each of her friends came and celebrated with her and hopes the night doesn't pass too quickly.

The Abduction

The party continues at the Rabeau's house with everyone having a good time and hoping nothing bad will happen until a familiar pick-up truck comes along.

Bruno: "Alright boys, you know the drill."

Cyprus: "Right. We search and seize the best looking ladies for our plan to lure Jackson out."

Louie: "This will be too easy, Bruno."

Kendall: "I am only here to get Riley back after that dhole furry punched my face in."

Bruno: "Dude forget her. We are here to grab Carina, Natasha, Amber, and that lynx girl Nova, who are all at this very moment in the Rabeau house as we speak."

Kendall: "How do you know this?"

Bruno: "I rigged an automated recon drone to survey the area before we parked on the other side of the block, bro. It's one of the Rabeau girl's birthday. Everyone's there for a party. I will go over this once more because we only have a short window of time to pull this off. We sneak around the mansion and just take them by force. By the time anyone figures out what happened and who is gone, we are outta there. Any more questions?"

The crew shakes their heads as a "No" response.

Bruno: "Good, now let's go acquire our targets."

Cyprus walks out in the unaware crowd after Amber while Kendall stalks after Nova.

Bruno: "Alright, Louie, you take Natasha, and I will take Carina."

Louie: "Got it."

Bruno: "Hi, Carina."

Carina: "What do you want, Bruno?"

Bruno: "That's no way to greet someone. Is it, Louie?"

Louie: "Definitely not, Bruno."

Natasha: "Let us go, you creeps!"

Louie: "Stop squirming, foxy girls."

Natasha and Carina bite their captors' arms and run outside to the back of the house where Kendall and Cyprus are waiting to knock them unconscious, using a customized anesthesia spray. The two are loaded into Bruno's truck.

Bruno: "Great job, boys. Now let's take them all back to the hideout for some entertainment."

.......One hour later.......

Taciana: "Hey Jacky, can you help me find Carina, please? I am worried something might have happened to her. It's been a long time since I've seen her."

Jackson: "Sure, anything to help."

Taciana: "Thank you."

Jackson: "Look at this. It's a ring and a patch of fur. It looks like a struggle occurred here and this fur is thick and brownish in coloration."

Taciana: "What are you saying, babe?"

Jackson: "She was kidnapped by multiple assailants."

Sophia: "It's Bruno and his crew, isn't it?"

Taciana: "He's responsible for this?"

Sophia: "Yeah, because he has a problem with not getting whatever and whomever he wants. In this case, Carina."

Jackson: "Well that can't stand; I am going out to look for them and bring her, and anyone else they took, back."

Warrick: "Hold on, my dhole brother; aren't you going to need some backup?"

Jackson: "No, I can't risk anyone here getting injured or beaten. I've got this."

Taciana: "You sure?"

Jackson: "I practiced numerous martial arts back when I was a human. Don't worry, Taciana. I can put those fools in their place."

Taciana: "Please be careful, Jacky."

Jackson: "Always will."

Sophia: "You will find them at the abandoned cabin a few miles outside of Glassbec."

Jackson: "Okay. Hold on, Carina. Here we go, Jackson the rescue."

Mission: Save the Girls

Jackson: "I hope I make it there in time before those fools do something to Carina."

.......Meanwhile in Bruno's Hideout.......

Carina: "Geez, what hit me?"

Nova: "Those four morons took us into this nasty cabin."

Bruno: "You calling my hideout nasty, lynx?"

Nova: "Yeah, that's exactly what I'm saying!"

Kendall: "Quiet!"

Nova: "Ow! That hurt!"

Bruno: "Anyways, you're all just pawns in our game of revenge against that Jackson Tontione everyone seems to find so appealing. Since our plan to wreck those houses didn't work, we are doing this instead. We're going to get even this way. When he comes to rescue you, we're all going to jump him and get rid of him, once and for all."

Natasha: "You guys are crazy!"

Amber: "Leave us alone, you horrible furry!"

Louie: "Hey, Cyprus."

Cyprus: "Yeah, Louie?"

Louie: "The arctic chick needs a lesson on keeping her mouth shut."

Cyprus: "With pleasure."

Amber: "You can't do this!"

Bruno: "Actually, yes we can."

Bruno: "Cyprus and Louie, time to get in place for the trap. Hehehe."

Kendall: "Hey Bruno, a car just drove up near the hideout."

Bruno: "It is obviously our guest of honor who's come to save precious lives."

Jackson: "A cabin with no sign, huh? This must be the place. Better to take them by surprise."

Jackson busts down the door and sees Carina and the other three girls tied up and gagged with cloth in their mouths.

Jackson: "Hang on, I am getting you four out here, okay?"

Suddenly Jackson is surrounded by Bruno's crew. Jackson delivers an uppercut to Louie and uses a swift roundhouse kick on Kendall. He's rushed by Cyprus.

Cyprus: "Got ya, dhole boy."

Jackson: "What the heck?"

Cyprus: "Ouch! Why you little!"

Bruno: "Hold it right there, Tontione! Come any closer and the girls get it."

Carina: "Jackson!"

Bruno: "Shut up."

Jackson: "You spineless coward. Let Carina and the others go!"

Cyprus: "You don't make the demands here."

Jackson: "How about a little wager?"

Kendall: "He wants to make a deal with us?"

Louie: "We're listening, dhole."

Jackson: "You, Bruno, and the other two bumbling buffoons you have can face off against me in a head on match."

Bruno: "What makes you think that we'll agree to that? Now get lost or we'll take your rabbit girlfriend for a nice hefty ransom. We're sick of you."

In a burst of rage, Jackson puts the smack down on Bruno, ultimately knocking two of his teeth out. Bruno groans from the pain and collapses.

Jackson: "Do not threaten my family or my friends ever again."

Louie: "No one beats up our band!"

Jackson: "Too slow."

Jackson evades and paralyzes Louie with a blow to the stomach. Quickly he brings down Cyprus with a few well-timed blows to his back and sides. Kendall quivers nervously as Jackson looks at him. Kendall runs out of the cabin and into Cyprus' truck to hide.

Jackson: "They are done. Are you four okay? Hang on, I'll untie you."

Carina: "I am now. Thank you so much."

Natasha: "Yeah."

Nova: "That was pretty incredible, Jackson."

Amber: "You can save me any day!"

Jackson: "It was the right thing to do. Now let's get back to the house."

Amber: "Oh my goodness, you are bleeding. Do you feel any pain?"

Jackson: "It's fine, Amber. I can make it back before it gets worse."

Amber: "Nova, could you check out his wound please?"

Nova: "Come here, Jackson."

Jackson: "It wasn't that bad, girls."

Nova: "Jackson, you need some bandages to cover that until you return home, okay?"

Jackson: "I did not see anything medical lying around in this dump."

Nova: "Here. I will wrap this around your arm."

She tears off the sleeves from Cyprus's unconscious body and quickly winds the makeshift bandage around Jackson's wound.

Jackson: "That is awesome! Are you hoping to be like a doctor or something?"

Nova: "Think of it more as a survival skill."

Jackson: "Well, despite your reasoning, I bet you would be a real pro at it, Nova."

Nova: "You are too kind, Jackson."

Natasha: "Um, guys?"

Carina: "Can we all go back home now, please? This place is so depressing."

Amber: "I'm right with you. The atmosphere of this cabin is just screaming with a severe need of refurbishment."

Jackson: "Oh, that's correct. It is time to go, ladies. You all ready?"

Amber: "This arctic fox is so ready!"

Jackson: "Alright then. Let's get rolling."

Gratitude Part I

As Jackson drives the four girls back to the Rabeau house, Carina watches as Nova takes long side glances at Jackson.

Carina: "Um, Jackson?"

Jackson: "Yeah."

Carina: "I have never seen anyone take on a whole gang solo, before."

Jackson: "Doing the right thing for others has always been a rewarding experience for me."

Carina: "Is there any way I can show my gratitude?"

Jackson: "You don't owe me anything, Carina."

Carina: "No, I just wanted you to know that I really appreciate the rescue. Many of us at school see you as the new local hero."

Jackson: "Awww, shucks. It was nothing."

Amber: "Are you kidding? You stood up for what is right and did everything you could to ensure our safety."

Carina: "You are definitely one of a kind, Jackson Tontione."

Nova: "Heroic deeds and enjoying yourself at a mansion party in one afternoon? Hugely impressive and it is the kind of thing that I am looking for in a future mate."

Jackson: "I just want to protect everyone who is good here."

Carina: "Why is that, Jackson?"

Jackson: "Back when I was human, others would make excuses or chicken out about trying to be a noble individual in society."

Carina: "That is horrible."

Jackson: "I can make a real difference here because the corruption of this world isn't as bad as the one I knew two thousand years ago."

Carina: "Well, I am glad you became a better man for it."

Carina smooches his ear from the back seat as Jackson parks his car. Jackson then opens the doors for all of them and receives a kiss on the cheek in gratitude from each of the furry girls. The five of them walk back into the Rabeaus' house to continue the party, but a lot of the guests are looking distraught until Taciana sees Jackson and her rescued friends safe and sound. Taciana rushes up to Jackson and presses her lips against his.

Taciana: "Jackson? Oh my goodness. Are you okay? How was the mission?"

Jackson: "I'm fine, Tacci, I am fine. I saved Carina and the others from that cabin."

Sophia: "What happened to Bruno and his crew?"

Jackson: "Let us just say they will never be messing with anyone around Glassbec for a long time."

Sophia: "Jackson, you are incredible!"

Carina: "He sure is."

Taciana: "Relax, everyone! My boyfriend and hero has returned!"

Crowd: "Jackson! Jackson! Jackson!"

Warrick: "Way to go, bro! Fist bump!"

Hours later, the party ends when the food is gone and everyone is too tired to dance anymore. Everyone heads home except for Renet and Carina, who want to help Jackson and the Rabeaus clean up the mess left behind.

Gratitude Part II

The next morning, everyone heads for school. Jackson stops to pick up Natasha on the way. Taciana is driving her new car, following closely, with Warrick just behind. The teenagers turn on the radio, listening to the newest hit song, Fling it Like a Furry. All of them are singing along, windows down, as the cars pull into the school's parking lot.

Natasha: "Well that was fast."

Jackson: "We beat the heavier traffic and that's what matters, Tasha."

Natasha: "Okay, I am gonna head inside for class even though no one is there. It is best to maintain my perfect attendance record."

Jackson: "That's the spirit. Let me lock the car."

Natasha: "So, I wanted to ask you something. I wanted to know if you were ready to change your mind about dating Taciana and choose me as your new number one choice?"

Jackson: "Natasha, you probably didn't overhear this, but my loyalty and faithfulness is to Taciana. I'm sorry."

Natasha: "I understand."

Jackson: "You do?"

Natasha: "My Dad taught me that loyalty and faithfulness come first in a relationship with the one you care about the most."

Jackson: "My former family from way before gave me the same advice many years ago. We're still good though, right? Friends?"

Natasha: "Of course. Always."

Warrick: "Alright, everybody. Let us get this day over with."

Renet: "Why the sour mood?"

Warrick: "I'm sour because it is Monday."

Renet: "Don't be pouty, War."

Warrick: "Who wouldn't be down on a Monday?"

Renet: "I'm not feeling down at all, bae."

Warrick: "How are you not?"

Renet: "I have you and you have me."

Ramona: "Let's go sisters. We have a lot to do and a lot to learn."

Walking into the school, they notice a few new furries who were waiting by the classrooms.

Tawny: "Who are those new guys?"

Ramona: "It's probably their first day. I would not bother talking to them now, we can meet them at lunch if they come over. That way we aren't late for class."

Serena: "One of them is watching me, Ramona."

Ramona: "Ignore him. We need to get to class on time."

Kumal: "Dude, I know it is our first day and all, but this school has some fine-looking ladies."

Mitchell: "Are you talking about those three rabbit furries?"

Kumal: "Well yeah. I don't mind the interspecies thing at all. Do you?"

Mitchell: "I got no problem with it at all, but our crew might not like the fact that we are trying to date rich girls."

Kumal: "How do you know they're rich?"

Mitchell: "The shiny bracelets and clothes they have on them."

Kumal: "We are both foxes and I have seen fox furries date rabbit furries before."

Mitchell: "Just hold off on that until the boss makes his decision on how things will go here, understand?"

Kumal: "Understood."

The students all take their seats. During morning announcements, they all cheer when the principal comes over the loudspeaker and congratulates them on the Flats for Furries project.

Principal: "And I'd especially like to thank you all for persevering when someone vandalized the homes. A special thank you also to our one formerly human student, Jackson, for his role in motivating us all and encouraging his classmates to finish the project, despite setbacks. Jackson, you are a true furry and a credit to your host family."

Students: "Three cheers for Jackson!"

Jackson: "Aw, just doing my part, everyone."

Taciana: "That's my furry man!"

.......7 hours and 30 minutes later.......

Jackson: "Well once again, classes are completely set up to test us, my Tacci."

Taciana: "You shouldn't be worried, baby."

Jackson: "Hehe, I guess that's just the small part of me I can't help."

Taciana: "I can help you, Jacky. We can go over all the homework you want tonight, okay?"

Jackson: "Thanks, Tacci."

Taciana: "I will wait for you when you come home."

The two trade kisses, then she winks and walks to her new car on the right side of the parking lot. They drive home, waving to each other at the traffic lights. After they grab a snack, they sit in the living room with their textbooks and notes.

Jackson: "Okay, so this is the one problem where we have to divide mass by volume?"

Taciana: "You are close, Jacky, but it's only the formula. First, we have to find the amounts that are given in the problem and we use that to our advantage to solve it."

Jackson: "Oh, okay I got it now."

Taciana: "What did you get for the answer?"

Jackson: "The result I came to was 0.26 for the density."

Taciana: "I got the same answer."

Taciana: "Great job, Jacky, we have completed the physics assignment for next week."

Jackson: "Yeah and it's only 7:00 pm."

Taciana: "Yup, that means more downtime. Hehehe."

Jackson: "I am going to go see an action film at the theater. Want to come?"

Taciana: "I can't, you go ahead. But first… Mmmwwah. There, a kiss. Now you can go."

Jackson: "Thank you, Taciana."

Taciana: "Have fun, babe."

Warrick: "Action film? Can I join?"

Jackson: "Sure, man! Let's go."

…….25 minutes later…….

Jackson and Warrick choose the closest parking spot to the front of the theater. There they see a group of friends from school.

Jackson: "There are no parking meters?"

Warrick: "No, they got torn out by the original furries who redesigned Glassbec."

Jackson: "Why?"

Warrick: "They had no real purpose as the town already makes more than enough money."

Jackson: "No toll fees for cars either, huh?"

Warrick: "There aren't as many, but there are a few on the way to the cities."

Jackson: "I never liked them back when I was human because they would cause a major traffic buildup on certain roads."

Warrick: "Don't worry, we have way more toll-free routes to use, Jackson."

Jackson: "So, what movie do you wanna watch? I was going to pick one of these action flicks. There's some good ones showing."

Warrick: "How about the Thundering Liger?"

Jackson: "That looks awesome! You have a good eye for films."

Warrick: "Follow me. Let's go buy automated tickets."

Jackson: "Wow, thirteen dollars and twenty-five cents per adult?"

Warrick: "That's not so bad. It was actually twenty-eight dollars and fifty cents last year, but they changed it to get more people in here."

Jackson: "This night just gets better. I hope the snacks are good too."

He inserts his debit card and chooses to pay with the credit option for two tickets.

Jackson: "Here we are, one for you and one for me."

Warrick: "Thanks. Popcorn and nachos are on me."

Jackson: "I'll get us some sodas. Movies and popcorn always make me thirsty."

Concessions Seller: "Anything else for you two?"

Warrick: "That's it! Showtime! Let's go, Jackson. Follow me. You got the tickets?"

Jackson: "Yes. Let me get them out of my pocket."

Ticket Handler: "Welcome."

Jackson: "We have two tickets for the Thundering Liger film, good sir."

Ticket Handler: "Theater nine on your left. Enjoy the show, folks."

.......2 hours and 30 minutes later.......

Jackson and Warrick are walking out of the theater when they see Tobias and Abby walk out. They stop to say hello.

Tobias: "How did you like the movie?"

Jackson: "It was fantastic."

Abby: "That movie really spoke to me."

Jackson: "How so?"

Abby: "Well, the hero, Thundering Liger, always came to the rescue of the beautiful lioness Antionette every time she was trapped."

Warrick: "Yeah, and what a hero he was! Made me think of Jackson, here."

Jackson: "Well guys, we got to go. See you in school tomorrow!"

Warrick and Jackson drive home. Jackson plans to practice a few of the moves from the movie. You never know when they will come in handy, he thinks.

The Survivalist: Trip Preparation

Nova: "No, please save me!"

Melody: "Sis, what's going on?"

Nova: "It's nothing, Melody. Just a messed-up nightmare."

Melody: "Do you want to talk about it?"

Nova: "Sniffle. I was back in the cabin with Bruno and his goons, but no one came for me and they just laughed at my misfortune!"

Melody: "Relax, Nova. It's over. You're safe."

Nova: "Yeah I know, I just can't get it out of my head."

Melody: "Okay, first of all, who rescued you?"

Nova: "It was Jackson. Jackson Tontione."

Melody: "You mean the cute dhole furry?"

Nova: "Yeah."

Melody: "Well there is your solution, big sister. Go find him and tell how you really feel and thank him in a way he will never forget."

Nova: "Okay, but there is just one issue."

Melody: "What's that?"

Nova: "He's dating Taciana."

Melody: "Oh well, I see how that can be problematic. Never thought you would go after a guy who is unavailable. Cheer up, sis, it's a brand-new day!"

Nova: "You are right. It is time to make the best of it. Plus, I think Jackson will love this survival outfit I created with my own two hands. I'll have to show him later."

The two head to the school bus stop, chattering all the way.

.......At the Rabeau's House.......

Taciana brushes her hair long and wraps it into a bun. She hums as she gussies up for the morning. Jackson watches her from the doorway. She catches sight of him and turns around smiling.

Taciana: "Hey, hun. Do you think you can sing for me one night in our room?"

Jackson: "Why? What brought this on?"

Taciana: "I just thought it would be a nice gesture if my boyfriend could lay down some jams."

Jackson: "I can sing, Tacci, it is just I need a little practice before I do."

Taciana: "I overheard you singing once, baby cakes."

Jackson: "That was just me imagining myself on stage, but I wouldn't take that kind of life."

Taciana: "We would be even more stable than we are now. There would be fans lining up to get your autograph and me standing next to you."

Jackson: "I cannot stand the thought of losing you to someone else because of my lack of giving you attention."

Taciana: "Honey, we will both get jobs in the future. Besides, we can have a duet if you want to on Saturday."

Jackson: "Okay."

Taciana: "I love you, Jacky."

Jackson: "I love you too, Tacci."

Jackson: "Your hair looks stunning as always, my sensational bunny girl."

Taciana: "Hehehe. Oh, am I? Such a strong and strapping dhole."

Jackson: "Yeah."

Mrs. Rabeau: "Kiddos! It is time for school!"

Taciana: "We are coming, Mama! Jacky, it is time to head out."

The two hold hands as they walk down the long staircase to the kitchen for some buttered toast.

Jackson: "Thank you, Mrs. Rabeau. Bye!"

Taciana: "Yeah, thanks Momma!"

Mrs. Rabeau: "Oh young love. Gets to me every time."

Ramona: "Morning, Mom."

Tawny: "Morning."

Serena: "Morning."

Warrick: "Good morning everybody!"

Mr. Rabeau: "Son, you don't have to holler it out every time before you leave the house this early. Use your inside voice. And save some of that blackberry jam for your sisters."

Warrick: "My bad, Pop."

Mr. Rabeau: "That's Dad to you."

Warrick: "Sorry, Father."

Mr. Rabeau: "Here is a celery sandwich and berry juice for school."

Warrick: "Thanks, Dad. Goodbye!"

Mrs. Rabeau: "You too, ladies. Go on. Don't be late."

The three sisters jump into the back of Warrick's truck, ready for the drive to school.

.......40 minutes later.......

Everyone arrives in time to hear the early bell ring.

Jackson: "It feels good to be right on time."

Taciana: "You could say that again."

Warrick: "Renet should be here, did you hear from her last night?"

Ramona: "Nope."

Tawny: "Nope."

Serena: "Nada."

Taciana: "Sorry, big bro."

Jackson: "Not sure if she called, man."

Warrick: "I better call her on my cell." RING, RING, "Renet, are you okay?"

Renet: "War baby, I am staying at home today."

Warrick: "What's wrong?"

Renet: "I have been feeling sick all morning."

Warrick: "Oh okay. I will bring you all the assignments from today and we'll go over them together."

Renet: "Sounds good."

Renet hangs up the phone and sits back down worried.

Renet: "I am over 100 degrees Fahrenheit! Hope my War doesn't catch what I have when he comes by. I better rest and have some soup."

.......At the school.......

Jackson: "Relax bud, she will be alright."

Warrick: "I hope so, bro."

Jackson: "You need to stay strong for her and do anything it takes to help her through it. If it was Taciana, I would fight no matter what."

Warrick: "Thanks, man."

Everyone starts walking into the school entrance, but Taciana stops Jackson before he walks in.

Taciana: "You would fight till the end for me?"

Jackson: "You overheard that, did you?"

Taciana: "Yeah, I overheard while I was chatting with my sisters about future goals."

Jackson: "You did ask me to be your future mate, bae."

Taciana: "Let us go to class, charmer boy. Don't want to be late, do you?"

Jackson: "We are always on time, sweetheart."

Evelyn: "Hey lovebirds, mind if we all join you during lunch?"

Taciana: "Of course, everyone's welcome. Right, handsome?"

Jackson: "Absolutely."

Abby: "I'm glad to have friends like you!"

Tobias: "Abby, as much as I enjoy seeing your smile, I don't want you to over excite yourself. You'll wear yourself out."

Abby: "Sorry Toby, it is just so great to be in a world where way more of us can get along than not. Better now?"

Tobias: "Hehehe, so cute and giggly."

.......12:00 pm - 1:00pm.......

Yahar: "Lunches are becoming a little stale these days."

Riley: "My lunch does not taste stale to me."

Yahar: "Riley, you only grabbed organic chicken nuggets and fruit."

Riley: "Go organic, my friend."

Yahar: "Still, I just prefer a nice meaty or crunchy lunch that has not been sitting in a school fryer for too long, is all."

Evelyn: "Yahar, be thankful that we get free lunches. There are some schools in and outside of Glassbec that do not give away free lunches."

Jackson: "What other towns are there outside of Glassbec?"

Evelyn: "Well, I know there is Norbury, they have these solar panels spread all over it."

Miles: "Glassbec has some solar panels here too, just not as many."

Jackson: "You must be Miles."

Miles: "Yup, that is me. Riley invited me."

Jackson: "It's nice to meet your new friend, Riley."

Riley: "Oh of course. Hehehe, not a problem, Jackson."

Amber: "Hey everyone! I have some exciting news!"

Sophia: "What is it?"

Amber: "I'm a big sister now!"

Taciana: "Aww, is it a boy or a girl?"

Amber: "It's a little boy."

Jackson: "What's the kid's name?"

Amber: "Romello. Little Romello."

Melody: "Well, we are happy for you Amber."

Sophia: "What's up with you two?"

Nova: "My sister was just reminding me that I have a day camping trip to plan after school today."

Jackson: "Why?"

Nova: "Well, it is something that is supposed to prove how well I can survive out in the natural elements."

Ava: "Is this like one of those "rite of passage" scenarios?"

Nova: "Yes, exactly. My parents say it is crucial to know survival skills in order to prepare for the unexpected while traveling."

Carina: "That doesn't sound very safe to go on alone, Nova."

Nova: "Which is why I need to ask if one of you could go on this trip with me and Melody."

The table is silent for a few minutes.

Jackson: "I will go."

Rabeau Sisters: "What?"

Ramona: "You want to go on a survival trip?"

Jackson: "Sure I don't mind going, it is just to keep Nova safe while she handles the trials that lie ahead in the Accreton Forest."

Nova: "You have done thorough research on the forest, right?"

Jackson: "Well not fully, but I am sure you know the way since you have been there before."

Nova: "Hmm, I guess we are both learning with the map my parents provided me."

Jackson: "You okay with this, Tacci?"

Taciana: "I don't know, Jacky, it could be dangerous."

Jackson: "It will be fine. I have gone to survival camps at a young age. It should be a piece of cake."

Taciana: "Okay, just promise me you will be extra careful, please?"

Jackson: "I promise that I will be extra cautious."

Taciana: "Good, I don't want anything bad to happen to my bae."

Abby: "You two are just so cute together, it just makes me cry a little."

Taciana: "Thank you, Abby."

Tobias: "I guess he is going with you, Nova."

Nova: "No one else volunteered, so yay! We will meet by your car after school, right?"

Jackson: "Sure."

Nova: "This is going to be fun and life changing."

.......2 hours and 48 minutes later.......

Taciana: "Okay, here are some camping supplies I bought for you at the school gift shop."

Jackson: "Making sure that I am prepared for the outdoors, huh?"

Taciana: "I know you are a natural at surviving, honey, but it never hurts to have extra supplies. Oh, and here is an extended range walkie talkie in case you need to contact me or if there is an emergency."

Jackson: "Alright Tacci, I will take them and use what is necessary, okay."

Taciana: "Be safe, baby!"

Jackson: "I will! Bye!"

He jumps in his car with Nova waiting on the passenger side and Melody in the back. During the drive back to their house,

Nova fixes up her binoculars for a 300 percent zoom adjustment.

Nova: "Tonight, we head out to traverse the Accreton Forest as true survivalists!"

Jackson: "I won't lie Nova; this does sound really cool."

Melody: "I like the outdoors, but I am more of a picnic at home kind of girl, Nova."

Nova: "No takebacks, sister. We drive over the second we are ready for this trip. One last thing. Jackson, I want you to give me your honest opinion on my state-of-the-art survival outfit."

Jackson: "It sounds like you are ready for the outdoors!"

The Survivalist: A Mutual Feeling

They reach Nova and Melody's house and strap on all the gear they will require for the trials of the forest. Nova poses like a supermodel in her outfit.

Nova: "Well, Jackson, how do I look?"

Jackson: "To be honest, your outfit looks well crafted."

Nova: "Thanks. Oh, I also have this for you."

Jackson: "A glow in the dark flashlight?"

Nova: "Of course, I mean all three of us are going to be in the forest for most of the night."

Melody: "Trust me, she will never stop insisting. Just take it. As for me, I would rather have Glassbec's hero prepared to fight anyone that is lurking out there."

Jackson: "Hehehe. Nova, I just do what I think is right."

Nova: "Don't ever degrade yourself, Jackson; you are a great hero to most of us."

Jackson: "Wow, I did not think I would end up feeling like the prince of a town, but I will take it."

Nova: "Is that what you think? You are a brave soul and no one can tell you differently."

Jackson: "Thanks, I appreciate the compliment, Nova."

Melody: "Let's go already!"

Nova: "Stop your whining, we have to follow the map, sis."

.......18 minutes later.......

The three of them walk to their designated campsite in the Accreton Forest after some sightseeing. After some effort, the three get the campsite set up.

Nova: "This is it! Now that camp has been set up, we can finally start the challenge."

Jackson: "Good. What is the challenge in this rite of passage, Nova?"

Nova: "The first one is called "Capture the Flag."

Jackson: "Oh, this sounds fun."

Melody: "Does this involve a lot of running?"

Nova: "Yes Melody, it involves running from one location to another. The goal is to start from our campsite on the map and snatch the flag from the pole before your opponent does. Whoever wins, picks the activity for the night."

Jackson: "Sounds fair."

Melody: "You are so on!"

Nova: "Excellent. Be back in a few!"

After some trekking up the hill, she sprays a lemon scent on the flag.

Nova: "Mmm. This scent shall be unmistakable during the race."

.......One hour later.......

Nova returns to the campsite.

Nova: "You ready to race?"

Melody: "Nova, you won't believe it!"

Nova: "What happened while I was gone?"

Melody: "Jackson saved me from a wild panther that attacked me."

Nova: "Geez Melody, do you need any medical attention?"

Melody: "No, no it's okay. He actually splinted my leg with cleaned off twigs, some old clothing, and a bandage from the first aid kit to patch me and the wild cat up."

Nova: "You helped, using only a very few natural elements?"

Jackson: "It wasn't hard, but yeah. Allow me to explain what happened."

Nova: "I'm all ears."

.......Flashback to 40 minutes ago.......

As the two chat, a large mountain lion uses the thick underbrush to stalk them as they talk.

Jackson: "Have you ever gone deep sea fishing before?"

Melody: "No, but I would like to give it a try."

Jackson: "I could show you how. All it requires is the right bait."

Melody: "But what if I fumble on it and the fish gets away?"

Jackson: "It's okay, I–Melody do not move. There is a panther lurking behind you."

Melody turns around and screams. The beast pounces on her as she tries to defend herself by spraying it with pepper spray, but the predatory hunter evades substance and just shakes it off. The wild panther growls and bites down on her left leg.

Melody: "Help me! Help! It is trying to eat me!"

Jackson: "Leave her alone!"

He jabs it in the backside with a handmade spear left by a previous camper. The panther growls out in pain and collapses from the wound. Jackson is about to finish it once and for all until he spies four cubs mewing after the bigger one.

Melody: "Jackson, wait. Don't kill it!"

Jackson: "Why? She tried to chew up your lower leg! I'm ending this!"

Melody: "You really wanna take her away from her cubs?"

Jackson looks at the cubs and sees the innocence in their eyes as they crawl over and lick their mother's wounds clean.

Jackson: "Yeah, alright. I personally wouldn't want to hurt a cub like that either."

He grabs some sticks and the first aid kit and covers Melody and the mother panther's wounds up to heal. Suddenly, to their surprise, the panther cubs walk and crawl on an exhausted Jackson and lick his face with their rough tongues.

Melody: "You did it. You patched us up."

Jackson: "Ugh, Melody, what are they doing?"

Melody: "Aww, that is so cute. I think they are thanking you for saving their Momma."

Jackson: "Okay, okay, you are welcome. Just stop licking me."

Melody: "It seems like they want to stay here with us."

Jackson: "Okay, I guess they stay at our camp."

The little cubs mew excitedly after hearing Jackson's decision. The mother panther went to sleep to regain her strength after the fight with our two campers.

Melody: "Nova is going to be shocked when she returns."

Jackson: "We'll explain everything in great detail to your sister. Don't worry, I got this."

.......Flashback Ends.......

Jackson: "And that is what took place during the time you were setting up the flag."

Nova: "Wow, that is amazing Jackson! You protected my sister, and you did not break the law of the forest by killing a protected species! Thank you so much. You really are the Hero of Glassbec."

Melody: "I know! Wait until everyone hears what happened."

Jackson: "Melody actually persuaded me into helping the panther instead of finishing it off."

Melody: "Are you saying I am a hero too?"

Jackson: "Yes."

Nova: "Do you think you can complete the rite of passage tonight?"

Melody: "No, not tonight, sis. I need to recover and keep an eye on these little cuties."

Nova: "Alright you rest up then, Mel. I guess Capture the Flag will only involve the two of us."

Jackson: "Seems that way."

Nova: "First one who makes it uphill to that flag in less than an hour, wins."

Jackson: "You ready?"

Nova: "Three, two, one, and go!!!"

Nova takes off quickly across the camping fields and on to the trail.

Jackson: "Hey no fair! You leaped before running! And you know where the flag is!"

Nova: "No rule against that, hero! Haha haha."

.......50 minutes later.......

They keep running up the rocky outcrops of the mountain and finally see the flag.

Jackson: "Oh snap, I have picked up the scent of a lemony flag. Yes!"

He follows the scent and reaches the flag and touches it three seconds before Nova runs up and grabs it.

Jackson: "Looks like I win."

Nova: "What! No, I grabbed the flag, so that means I win."

Jackson: "I touched it a few seconds before you did; so that means I am the winner."

Nova: "Call it a tie?"

Jackson: "Fine, let's call it a tie. Only because that thing you do with those blue eyes is kinda adorable."

Nova: "What thing with my eyes?"

Jackson: "The whole sad and pleading eyes routine, Nova."

Nova: "It works, doesn't it?

Jackson: "Yeah, I will give you that one."

Nova: "Jackson?"

Jackson: "Yes, Nova?"

Nova: "I have to tell you something. It is something I should have told you before when you rescued me."

Jackson: "What is it? You can trust me."

Nova: "Ever since I found out about you, I have been curious."

Jackson: "What do you find curious about me?"

Nova: "The tenderness and care you show to others even if you have not spent that much time with them before. It is remarkable."

Jackson: "It is better to try and make friends with somebody new, even if that person doesn't seem like they want to be friends."

Nova: "I never took you for a wisdom type of guy."

Jackson: "I am full of surprises, survival girl. What should we do now?"

Nova: "We should head back to camp."

Jackson: "I thought we were gonna explore a little bit?"

Nova: "Well, I do know about this secret grove that is not too far from our campsite."

Jackson: "How far is it exactly?"

Nova: "Oh, it is approximately thirteen hundred and twenty feet away from here."

Jackson: "Alright, then lead the way to this special grove."

.......A short time later.......

Nova: "Step into the open and you will see why I love this spot so much."

Jackson steps into the field and thousands of fireflies are glowing unusually bright in the afternoon sky.

Jackson: "Nova, you were right. This place is pretty special."

Nova: "I told you."

Jackson: "I have never seen this many fireflies in one place or even move together like that. Especially during the day."

Nova: "It is because their population is the most balanced in this spot of the forest."

The two watch for a while, until Jackson's stomach starts growling.

Jackson: "Let's head back. I'm hungry."

Nova: "Here, have a survival bar. They aren't too bad."

Jackson: "You are right, this is pretty tasty."

Nova: "There will be plenty more of where that came from after we walk back home from camp."

She takes his paw and leads him back towards the campsite and notices Melody with the four panther cubs asleep all around her.

Nova: "Awww, that's so cute! They think she is a part of their family."

Jackson: "Well, just to be sure there is no bad blood between me and the big carnivore I bought this in case I got hungry during our walk to the grove. I liked your survival bar better though."

He takes out a piece of steak. The mother panther, however, doesn't want to leave the cubs and apparently likes Melody's company. The mother panther licks Melody's cheek and her cubs. The big cat growls threateningly at Jackson.

Jackson: "Easy now, I am not going to hurt you anymore."

He moves closer with the steak and offers it to her slowly while giving her eye contact. The mother panther clamps on to the steak and eats it, leaving only the T-bone behind.

The panther purrs and rubs up against his paw, thus accepting his presence.

Nova: "She thinks you are okay to be around."

Melody: "Can we take them with us?"

Jackson: "No we cannot take them from their home, Melody."

Melody: "Aww, but little Chip keeps following me."

Nova: "You named one of the cubs?"

Melody: "Yeah. Why can't I?"

Nova: "Last time you kept one of the regular carnivores of the forest, it attacked Mom and ran out of the kitchen window."

Melody: "Hey, I did not know that was going to happen, Nova!"

Jackson: "Calm down, you two. You are making the panther mom nervous."

Nova and Melody: "Sorry."

Melody: "Can I at least hug them goodbye before we go?"

Nova: "Go ahead."

Melody: "Take care of yourselves, okay?"

She hugs the cubs and the mother panther as they purr in response. Then the mother panther heads back into the woods and up towards her mountainous cave entrance with her cubs to rest.

.......18 minutes later.......

Nova: "We are back, Mom."

Mrs. Sudina: "How was your survival trip?"

Nova: "It was the best one ever!"

Mrs. Sudina: "Why are you limping? What happened to your leg?"

Melody: "We tamed a wild panther."

Mrs. Sudina: "Melody, I told you to not go anywhere near the wild ones! You could have been killed by that panther."

Melody: "I'm fine, Mom. It was a big misunderstanding because the panther mistook me for a threat."

Mrs. Sudina: "So what, you made friends with it now? It is not a pet, honey."

Melody: "I know it is not. I noticed her four cubs were nearby. She was protecting her cubs and thought we were a problem."

Mrs. Sudina: "Well, regardless of what took place, I'm glad you're okay. Oh, hello. You are Jackson, right?"

Jackson: "Yes, Ma'am."

Mrs. Sudina: "You saved my little girls today. Thank you."

Jackson: "It was nothing, Mrs. Sudina. Well, I've got to go, but I'll see you later."

A Melodious Picnic

Dawn beams down on the guest cottage and the sun glares over our hero as he stretches his arms out with a yawn.

Jackson: "Good morning, sun. It is now an incredible Wednesday! I wonder what's on the breakfast menu? Maybe I should go and make it for everyone as a surprise."

Jackson sneaks into the main house and starts cooking breakfast. Soon everyone is greeted with a large breakfast of boiled eggs, sausage, and toasted homemade waffles.

Jackson: "Alright, that looks deliciously good."

Taciana and Warrick are the first to arrive and tuck in.

Warrick: "Thanks, man. This is great."

Taciana: "You are so sweet, my handsome dhole."

Serena: "Yum!"

Ramona: "You are so thoughtful, Jackson!"

Tawny: "I want the last waffle!"

Serena: "No, I want it!"

Ramona: "No, me!"

Taciana: "Guys, there's enough for everyone."

Jackson: "That's right! There is."

The furries begin eating breakfast and as they reach the last hard-boiled egg on the center plate, Jackson cracks the top and splits the soft interior with Warrick.

There is a knock at the back door, and everyone looks up to see Melody on her phone. She looks upset. Taciana opens the door to let her in. Melody's phone is on speaker phone, so everyone can hear.

Melody: "Look Caldenazo, I will bring the usual to lunch for me and you, okay?"

Caldenazo: "Good, and make sure it is fresh!"

She takes a seat at the table, Nova trailing in quietly and sighs sadly as Serena pushes over a waffle to each of them.

Jackson: "Who was that on the phone with you, Melody?"

Melody: "My boyfriend, Caldenazo."

Ramona: "Is he treating you right?"

Melody: "He yells at me when I don't get him the lunch he wants because he hates school lunches."

Jackson: "Why don't you tell him to find his own lunch and not sponge off you like that?"

Melody: "I have tried that, but it only makes him angry and I feel bad for him. I am going to school early. I just wanted to stop by and thank you again for helping me yesterday."

Taciana: "Wait a minute, you can ride to school with us."

Nova: "That would be great! It's a long walk."

Melody: "Thank you, guys!"

The sisters walk out the door and climb into Jackson's car to wait for the others. Jackson and Taciana ready their own bags and head towards the car.

Jackson: "Ready to roll?"

Taciana: "Sure am!"

Melody: "Sure."

Jackson: "Another great day at school!"

.......At the High School.......

Jackson: "So what are your two favorite classes, Nova?"

Nova: "Gym class and biology. You?"

Jackson: "Gym class and physics."

Nova: "Hmm, well if you ever want to join me for a workout, just call me up and we could go on an exercise regimen together."

Jackson: "That works. I will definitely call you about a possible meet up date."

Nova: "Hehehe. Cool."

Melody: "Were you serious about always having our backs if we need your help?"

Jackson: "Yeah, I gave my word."

Melody: "You are a good furry, Jackson. Talk to you later."

Jackson: "Yeah, anytime."

.......Lunchtime ....

As everyone reached the lunch table, they noticed that Nova was there without Melody.

Taciana: "Hey Nova! Isn't Melody going to join us?"

Nova: "She said Caldenazo wanted some alone time with her."

Taciana: "I've heard a story about Caldenazo."

Jackson: "What kind of story?"

Taciana: "He got suspended last year for beating her up right after she rejected his offer to prom."

Jackson: "That is not right, no one should beat anyone up over a little rejection. And you should never hurt anyone like that."

Taciana: "You are absolutely right, Jackson. I wish there was a way to make everyone good like you."

Jackson: "Aww, Tacci, that is just the gentleman in me."

Taciana: "How was the trip yesterday, Jacky?"

Jackson: "It was fun. In fact, me and Nova raced up to the highest mountain in the Accreton Forest."

Taciana: "Did you win?"

Jackson: "I would have been the winner if the terrain was not so rugged."

Nova: "You wish. I was a few seconds behind him, but we touched the flag at the same time."

Jackson: "She leaped at the beginning of the race and then leaped to reach the flag when I ran towards it."

Nova: "Guilty."

Taciana: "Even though it was a tie; I am glad the two of you are unharmed."

Nova: "Thanks, Taciana. It means a lot."

Taciana: "Of course."

Pepper: "Jackson? What happened to Melody's left leg?"

Jackson: "We had a little trouble with a wild panther that tried stalking us for food, but I fought it off and injured the beast."

Gulani: "Oh my goodness! There are still wild ones out there in Accreton?"

Jackson: "Indeed. Melody found out the hard way, but in the end I patched her and the beast up since the panther had cubs trailing behind her."

Everyone at the table looks at him in shock and surprise since they had never seen many wild ones come too close to furries before.

Riley: "I am assuming that you let the panthers live?"

Jackson: "Yes, because in that moment, Melody taught me that the panther's life is precious."

Miles: "You got wisdom, bro. I respect that."

Riley: "That's so cool."

Taciana: "Ahem."

Riley: "What? He's a hero."

Taciana: "Yeah, but he is still my boyfriend and not yours, Riley. Keep yourself under control."

Riley: "Hmmph."

Jackson: "Warrick, how is Renet doing?"

Warrick: "She is doing better, actually."

Jackson: "That's great news! She is going to need you more than ever."

Warrick: "Thanks, man. She called earlier and said she will come tomorrow."

…………Out in the hallway…………

Melody: "Look Calden, I don't want you to take this the wrong way, but can't you get your own food?"

Caldenoza: "Melody, you don't understand at all, do you?"

Melody: "Understand what?"

Caldenoza: "Let me remind you!"

He grabs her by the hair.

Melody: "Owww! Stop it!"

Suddenly something knocks the bobcat out.

Melody: "Jackson?"

Jackson: "Sorry Mel, I couldn't stand overhearing that situation. So, I stopped it from escalating even further."

Melody: "Is he…?"

Jackson: "He's fine, he's just knocked out."

Melody: "I appreciate the backup."

Jackson: "You're welcome."

Melody: "All of that got me thinking, maybe you are the one who can change this school for the better."

Jackson: "How so?"

Melody: "You can make a donation to Wild Eye High School to increase security around here to prevent future bullying and abuse."

Jackson: "That's a thoughtful idea Melody. I will think about it. Hey, why don't we do a fundraiser? Everyone can chip in. Maybe we can do a bake sale or something."

Melody: "Good idea! You know, I have never really met anyone as thoughtful and considerate as you."

Jackson: "First time for everything, right?"

.......In the School Courtyard.......

Mitchell: "I took a picture of the whole lunchroom and Salvador called me about taking everyone in the photo that this Jackson guy has been hanging out with."

Kumal: "Wait a minute, that is his plan? That is crazy, I was hoping to just ask one of the rabbit girls on a date. I don't want to force them into anything."

Marino: "Mitchell, I think Kumal has gone soft and has forgotten our true mission here."

Kumal: "I haven't gone soft; I was only thinking of a different way of keeping Clawtooth Clan pure and not corrupt."

Mitchell: "The only way that our crew is going to grow is if we have some ladies to expand it with."

Kumal: "What if they don't want to agree to our terms?"

Marino: "Then we force them to do what we want."

Kumal: "Fine, I guess this is how it has to be."

Mitchell: "That's more like it, now come on. It's class time."

.......The evening.......

Dinner is over, and Taciana, Jackson, Melody, and Nova are outside watching the stars. Jackson just finished explaining his idea of a summer fundraiser and everyone had agreed to spearhead some part of the plan. Jackson falls back on the ground, staring at the stars in the night sky.

Jackson: "I am glad the constellations never changed. It's good some things are still the same."

Melody: "My favorite constellation as a little lynx was always Gemini because I used to think me and my sister looked exactly the same."

Jackson: "Mine was Orion, since as a little guy I dreamed of being a bounty hunter with loyal fighters at my side."

Nova: "How are you so popular?"

Jackson: "The trick is to stay true of heart, by not losing yourself and not stooping down to the level of an individual with malice."

Taciana: "You sound like my grandfather."

Jackson: "I know that sounded deep, but it is true. You can ask anyone."

Melody: "Okay."

Taciana: "I'm glad your pod landed here, Jackson."

Nova: "Me too. You are making our town a safer and better place with all you've done to help."

Jackson: "I'm enjoying it too."

The teenagers chat a while longer before going their separate ways to their homes.

.......At 3:00 am in the morning.......

A terrible plan is already in motion. An assailant comes in through the open window and drags Melody off the bed.

Melody: "Let me go, you horrible heathen!"

Mitchell: "Keep your mouth shut, kitty."

He puts a chloroform-laced rag over her mouth to keep her quiet. Her muffled screams fade as slowly her eyes close.

Mitchell: "Okay she is out. Put her in the truck with the rest of them."

Marino: "Got her. Where is the other one?"

Mitchell: "The other lynx girl?"

Marino: "Yes, the other one."

Mitchell: "Kumal already carried her to the back of the truck. Were you even awake when that happened?"

Marino: "No, I just figured it would take him forever since Kumal is not as tough as we are when it comes to these types of missions."

Mitchell: "Kumal might be a bit of a sap, but you can count on him as muscle for the crew."

Marino: "You are both fox furries and I am a coyote furry. Toughness is something that we cannot let up with in this town."

Mitchell: "I know. Salvador taught us that."

Kumal: "Are we done?"

Marino: "Not yet. We still have a few more targets to hit this morning before the sun comes up."

Kumal: "Then what?"

Marino: "The boss man will fill us in on the rest of the details."

Mitchell: "Well, what are we standing around for? We got a neighborhood to raid."

The Ferocious Intervention

A seemingly peaceful morning approaches every one of the main households in Glassbec. As dawn shapes, three shadowy figures lurk in the darkness. Kumal, Mitchell, and Marino spent hours breaking into households and kidnapping everyone Jackson knows and cares about. So far Warrick, Tobias, Yahar, Miles, Ramona, Serena, Tawny, Ava, Gulani, Riley, Pepper, Evelyn, Abby, Renet, Sophia, Carina, Natasha, Amber, Nova, Melody, Tia, and little Romello are all currently asleep from the chloroform and are about to be transported to the Clawtooth Clan's lair. Their boss Salvador calls to inform them of the hostages and their usefulness.

Salvador: "Did you three get them all?"

Marino: "Yeah boss, we caught them."

Salvador: "Good, now bring them to me."

Marino: "Roger that."

Marino: "Okay that is all of them on the list."

Mitchell: "The boss is gonna be real glad with the haul we got."

Kumal: "Then let's deliver them already. We can't spend too much time out here because the Task Force starts patrolling in a couple of hours."

Mitchell: "He is right. Onward to Vandori Woods, my brethren!"

.......At 6:30 am in the morning.......

Jackson: "Huh. Where is everyone? The whole house is empty.

Slowly he looks around and calls out for Taciana and her sisters with deep concern. When there is no answer, he follows the sound of a sudden scream. It's Mrs. Rabeau.

Jackson: "Where are Taciana and her sisters?"

Mr. Rabeau: "We found this letter on the front door this morning."

Jackson: "Jackson, if you ever want to see all of your friends again, meet us down by the Vandori River close to the mountainside. Salvadore of the Clawtooth Clan."

Mrs. Rabeau: "What are you thinking?"

Jackson: "I am thinking that I'm going to save your daughters and all of my friends from this so-called Clawtooth Clan tonight."

Jackson's phone rings and he picks it up.

Taciana: "Jacky!"

Jackson: "Tacci, what's wrong? Are you okay?"

Taciana: "There is a bobcat furry in the guest house and he is trying to hurt me!"

Jackson: "A bobcat furry? Did you recognize him, babe?"

Taciana: "No, I couldn't tell. Please hurry!"

Jackson: "I'm coming, sweetheart! Just hold on!"

Jackson enters the guest cottage. He sees the assailant with a knife in his hand.

Assailant: "Just hold still girlie. I will make this quick."

Taciana: "Somebody help me!"

Jackson: "Hey you! Drop the knife now."

Assailant: "Fine."

Jackson: "Hiyah!"

Jackson sweeps the assailant's legs right from under him.

Taciana: "Oh Jackson. He tried to..."

Jackson: "Hey, it's okay now. I'm here."

Taciana: "Mmmwwah. I was so scared, but I'm glad you came for me, Jacky."

Jackson: "Now, it is time to question this guy about where the others are."

Assailant: "What in the world? Release me now!"

Jackson: "Here is what is going to happen, crook. You are going to tell me where the rest of my family and friends are right now!"

Assailant: "I won't tell you anything!"

Jackson then punches the assailant's stomach and takes off his mask.

Jackson: "Caldenoza?"

Caldenoza: "Yes, I am a member of the Clawtooth Clan and we are taking Glassbec back piece by piece, starting with Wild Eye High. We're gonna turn it into our kinda town. Where we run it, and everybody does what we say."

Jackson: "Not if I stop their uprising first."

Caldenoza: "You stole my Melody from me, so I joined up to get even and to help my crew gain true power."

Jackson: "I protected her from your senseless abuse."

Taciana: "Besides, my Jacky is always doing the right thing for others."

Jackson: "I appreciate that, Tacci."

Taciana: "You, on the other hand, are just part of a selfish pack of cowards who know nothing about respecting their fellow furries."

Caldenoza: "You just act so high and mighty because your family is rich."

Jackson: "My girlfriend's family has worked very hard to attain their wealth by maintaining their businesses in an honest manner. So yeah, you don't know anything about us at all."

Taciana: "Aww, sweetie. You can expect a big zesty reward after saving everyone."

Jackson: "I just don't want you to get hurt, babe."

Taciana: "Don't worry, honey, I will be fine. I am just going to have the staff to lock down the windows and exits after you leave."

Jackson: "First, I will have to take this lowlife to the Task Force Headquarters."

Jackson puts the tied up Caldenoza in the back seat of the car.

Taciana: "Please be cautious, honey."

Jackson: "I shall return with everyone right behind me, Tacci."

Taciana: "You better."

Caldenoza: "Just take me away so I can laugh about what my compatriots are currently doing to your friends."

Jackson: "Oh don't worry, you'll get your wish."

.......At the Task Force Headquarters.......

Quentin: "Morning team! What do we have on the teen furry disappearances from last night?"

Viscalli: "Captain Riles, we have no footage of the suspects because they most likely avoided the cameras on the streets."

Quentin: "We gotta have something!"

Ramirez: "Sir, someone is coming to the front door."

Quentin: "Who is it?"

Ramirez: It's one of those high school kids with another one tied up."

Quentin: "Let's see what he wants."

An automated door opens up and Jackson pushes Caldenoza in and introduces himself.

Jackson: "I am Jackson Tontione, and I need your help."

Quentin: "Help with what?"

Jackson: "According to this letter, the others were taken by the Clawtooth Clan to the Vandori River."

Quentin: "The Vandori River? Ramirez, wasn't that area abandoned ten years ago due to periodic rockslides?"

Ramirez: "Indeed. However, some of our scouts have observed increased Clawtooth activity in that sector."

Quentin: "Okay, radio the scouts and tell them to hold their positions."

Ramirez: "Yes, sir."

Ramirez: "Collins and Temroe, what is your status?"

Collins: "Still here, sir. Salvador's crew have already moved the hostages to his den."

Ramirez: "Alright, send us your coordinates and we will be on our way to assist."

Temroe: "You got it."

Ramirez: "Excellent, Ramirez out. Got some hot intel for you, Captain."

Quentin: "It is seven miles west of town. Grab your gear boys! We roll out in five minutes!"

The whole building rushes to the armory with regular guns, non-lethal tranquilizer guns, and batons.

Jackson: "What about this guy?"

Quentin: "Viscilli!"

Viscilli: "Yes, sir?"

Quentin: "Toss Caldenoza into a six by eight prison cell. I'll question him after we capture Salvador and his other associates."

Jackson: "Can I come too?"

Quentin: "No way, kid. This is a task force operation and you might get yourself hurt."

Jackson: "You don't understand. The letter said if I don't show up then they'll execute my friends. You have to take me with you to help."

Quentin: "Fine you can come, but that doesn't mean you're using any guns."

Jackson: "Can I at least have a stun baton?"

Quentin: "Permission granted."

Jackson: "Thanks."

Quentin then jumps in his SUV and turns on the high-pitched alarm up top and signals the others to rev up their engines.

Jackson: "This is so awesome!"

Quentin: "Viscilli, get the troops rolling!"

Viscilli: "On it, sir! Roll out people!"

The whole Task Force, along with Jackson their protégé, drive into the Vandori Woods and set up a perimeter at a safe distance.

Quentin: "Everyone, Temroe and Collins should be holed up nearby. Ramirez, scout ahead and report what you find. Understood?"

Ramirez: "I understand, Captain."

Ramirez goes off with tranquilizer gun in hand and crouches down by the river bank to spy on the enemy.

Ramirez: "Captain Riles, I have a visual of four guards by Salvador's cabin and I can see where they are holding the hostages."

Quentin: "Good."

Quentin: "Team one, get into position for the attack."

Jackson: "I am coming too."

Quentin: "I don't think that is a good idea, kid."

Jackson: "What? But you said I could help."

Quentin: "You did help us, by locating where your friends are."

Jackson: "I can handle myself in a fight, sir."

Quentin: "There is no talking you out of this, is there?"

Jackson: "I have family in there too, and I will not just stand idly by knowing they need my help."

Quentin: "Alright, you can come. However, you are sticking with me."

Jackson: "Deal."

Salvador: "Move the prisoners inside my cabin, boys."

Mitchell: "Yes, sir."

Marino: "Sure thing, boss man."

Ramona: "You don't have to do this. There is a better way to live your life."

Mitchell: "Quiet. We are going to make a crap ton of money off of you and your friends."

Warrick: "Hey! Hey! Point that at me and see what happens!"

Mitchell fires the pistol at the ground.

Mitchell: "You better keep your yap shut before I blow it off."

Kumal: "Mitchell, come on man there is no need for torture or hurting anyone."

Mitchell: "Kumal, this is how the crew has always done things. We take the girls as future mates and use them as leverage if they don't agree."

Kumal: "I'm just saying that–"

Marino: "Kumal, are you with us or against us?"

Kumal: "I am with you one hundred percent."

Marino: "Good, now guard them while I call up the rest of the clan to prepare the ritual."

Salvador leaves the cabin and summons every other member of the clan to a meeting spot down by the river. Over one hundred members, which include bear, wolf, coyote, fox, badger, wolverine, and weasel furries, wait for their leader.

Salvador: "Clawtooth Clan, tonight we shall spark the revolution against the local Glassbec government and tear down the oppressive establishments that have robbed us of our original way of life! We will take back what is ours. We will rule our way. However, to expand our collective we shall require numerous mates and muscle to satisfy our rise to power!"

Clawtooth Clan Members: "Yeah! Yeah! Yeah!"

One of the crowd spots Scout Collins and starts firing at him.

Collins: "Captain they are on to us! Start the assault."

Quentin: "You heard him, men. Attack!"

The bullets and tranquilizer darts start flying as blows begin on both sides of the battle between the GTF and CTC. Meanwhile, Kumal was suddenly starting to think about his life decisions and that he should reconsider his position.

Tobias: "I saw the look on your face when they said you wanted things to be different here."

Kumal: "You do not know anything about me and we are not similar!"

Tawny: "Come on dude, we can see it all over your face."

Serena: "Just let us go and we will show you a way to a better life."

Kumal: "You are just trying to rattle my chain with false promises, aren't you?"

Abby: "We are not trying to trick you, Kumal."

Evelyn: "Come on, listen to them. Try to think this through for yourself and not what this group of psychos tells you."

Yahar: "Come on man, we are trying to be reasonable here."

Mitchell and Marino head over and move Tia and Romello into the cabin for later use.

Amber: "Romello!"

Sophia: "Tia!"

Tia: "Sophie!"

Amber: "You monsters!"

Riley: "Jackson will save us, right?"

Miles: "We are gonna have to fight if we intend to escape."

Nova: "I hope we will."

Suddenly a tranquilizer dart hits Kumal's backside and he collapses.

Ava: "Wait, what was that?"

Carina: "Oh my goodness, it's Jackson!"

Jackson: "Hey guys, are you all okay?"

Pepper: "Much better now that you are here."

Gulani: "You need to cut off our restraints and save Tia and Romello."

Jackson: "Where are they?"

Natasha: "One of them moved Tia and Romello into the cabin."

Jackson: "For what purpose?"

Natasha: "I am not sure."

Sophia: "Please save them, Jackson."

Jackson: "I will as soon I free you all.

.......In Salvador's cabin.......

Tia: "You big meanies! You can't do this!"

Mitchell: "Keep It down you little brat, don't make me shoot you or the little whiner over there."

Tia: "No, please don't!"

Mitchell: "Boo hoo, who is going to stop me?"

Jackson swiftly electrocutes him with his stun baton and checks his pulse to make sure he is still alive.

Jackson: "Phew, all good."

Tia: "Jackson, you saved us!"

Jackson: "Glad you are okay, kiddo. Where is Romello?"

Suddenly Marino comes out of nowhere and grabs Tia, holding her at gunpoint.

Marino: "Put down the kid or the runt here gets it! Put your paws up right now!"

Jackson: "Unbelievable. We can settle this peacefully."

Marino: "After what you did to Kumal and Mitchell? I don't think so. This isn't a time for negotiation, only action!"

Jackson throws his stun baton at Marino's head and Tia runs out of the cabin back to Sophie. Jackson and Marino throw each other against the wall and exchange body blows. Jackson hits an old wound on Marino's stomach, which opens and bleeds.

Marino: "Ahhhh!"

Jackson finally knocks him unconscious with no problem. He walks outside and finds everyone recovering from the trauma of this unfortunate event. Ava hugs him first before anyone else.

Jackson: "That was rough. But at least you all are safe."

Ava: "You are number one in my book!"

Jackson: "Thanks, Ava."

Sophia: "Oh Tia, I'm so glad you're okay."

Tia: "Jackson is my hero."

Sophia: "Well he is my hero too."

Jackson: "Not a problem."

Amber: "Where is Romello?"

Jackson: "Don't worry Amber, I will get him."

Jackson picks him up from the cabin and hands him over to Amber.

Amber: "My sweet little brother! Are you alright?"

Everyone joined in for a group hug after Captain Riles went up the hill to tell them that the fight was over and the last of the CTC surrendered.

Quentin: "Let's bring you all home. Ramirez! Call the coroner for the bodies. We will have a funeral for some of our fallen brothers."

Ramirez: "Yes, sir."

Collins and Temroe walk up to Quentin saying that they have all the remaining members of the CTC in handcuffs except for Salvador.

Quentin: "Salvador vanished without a trace again?"

Temroe: "I am afraid so, sir."

Quentin: "Dang it. Okay, we will continue the search for him tomorrow, but for now we are going back to headquarters."

Jackson: "Come on guys, it has been a long day and I am famished."

Melody: "You are not the only one."

Natasha: "Such a terrifying intervention."

Quentin and his team then drove Jackson and his friends back to Glassbec while the transport teams take the suspects to prison.

The Poem

Taciana storms into the guest cottage, her hands on her hips.

Jackson: "What have I done?"

Taciana: "You took too much risk last night. You could have been killed!"

Jackson: "I was careful!"

Taciana: "No you weren't. I watched the news this morning. There was video all over. You are a hero, but at what cost? How long before one day you don't come back to me? Sometimes I think you'd rather be everyone's hero, instead of my boyfriend."

Taciana runs off crying. Jackson follows her into the kitchen, where she's sniffling.

Warrick: "You got yourself in quite the pickle there, brother."

Jackson: "Is there an easy way to reconcile with her and win her back?"

Warrick: "There is one way for you to cheer her up and maybe win her affection again."

Jackson: "What is it? I am up for trying anything at this point."

Warrick: "You can make a poem for her, but it can't be from your head, you have to create one from your heart."

Jackson: "Okay, I'll try that."

He heads up to his room to start thinking of an apologetic poem to give to Taciana.

.......2 hours later.......

Jackson: "This will no doubt get her attention. I am a genius! Plus, it is from the bottom of my heart."

He goes down into the kitchen where Taciana is crying and drinking a soda alone.

Taciana: "What do you want?"

Jackson: "Tacci, I am truly sorry for what I did. I don't expect you to forgive me, but at least hear me out with this poem I created for you. I hope you like it."

.......Beginning of the Poem.......

A Binding Love

Love that binds can be a blessing,

It's great in times of abundance,

Love that binds can lead to change,

It's tough in times of conflict,

No matter where, love stands strong,

Love that binds us can never break,

For you are one who saved me from oblivion,

Love that binds can lead to a full heart,

It flows through my mind and like the sea,

One could never dream in a life without you.

.......End of the Poem.......

Taciana: "That is the most sweetest thing anyone has ever given me!"

Jackson: "I promise I won't ever hurt you like that again. I don't mean to scare you, I just want to help others. I'm not trying to be a hero, it just happens."

Taciana: "Aww, I cannot stay mad at you. I forgive you, Jackson."

Jackson: "Does this mean you still want me around?"

Taciana: "Yes Jacky, I still want you around."

Taciana: "I love you, Jackson Tontione."

Jackson: "I love you too, Taciana Rabeau."

They looked into each other's eyes and held paws like the rest of their surroundings did not matter. Only the bliss of that single point in time.

Jackson: "Stereo, play us a slow song by Soul Tiger."

Device Voice: "Playing song."

They slow danced for a while; never breaking eye contact with each other.

Jackson: "Wow, your eyes really are blue as the sky. I could get hypnotized."

Taciana: "You are getting better at being romantic."

Jackson: "Not only that, but your hair looks like the one of a goddess."

Taciana: "Hehehe, this is only one of my major hairstyles."

Jackson: "Well, you are still the alluring bunny girl who saved me regardless of your hair style choices."

Taciana: "Oh, Jackson."

Claw Toothed Comeback

Taciana: "Oh Lala. So ready for a new day."

Jackson: "Looking good, Tacci."

Taciana: "Let's go handsome. I can smell breakfast."

Jackson: "It is going to be a fruit bowl, waffles, and sausage links."

Jackson: "This is going to be delicious."

Taciana: "You can have all the sausage babe, since the others and I don't eat meat."

Jackson: "I figured."

Taciana: "You are okay with that?"

Jackson: "Of course I am, Tacci."

Taciana: "You wanna share some of the fruit with me?"

Jackson: "Sure."

Saba: "Good morning, you two!"

Taciana: "Good morning, Momma."

Jackson: "Morning, Mrs. Rabeau."

Saba: "Sausage and waffles for Jackson and a large fruit bowl for you, Taciana."

Taciana: "Thanks."

Jackson: "Looks great!"

Warrick: "Good morning. How did yesterday go, sis?"

Taciana: "Jackson and I are going to be okay."

Jackson: "No worries here, bro."

Ramona: "Good morning to all! Especially you, stud master."

Jackson: "Ramona, the bunny girl of my dreams is already next to me."

Taciana: "You tell them, sugar."

Ramona: "Whatever."

Jackson: "Not a chance."

Serena: "Excuse me? He actually cares about me more than you!"

Tawny: "In your dreams."

Saba: "There is no shouting allowed at the table."

Bolton: "Girls! That is enough. This young man has already made his choice and they have my blessing."

Taciana: "Really Daddy? Me and my Jacky can get married one day?"

Bolton: "Of course."

Taciana: "Jacky, will you promise to surprise me when you pop the question?"

Jackson: "I solemnly swear, my Tacci."

Taciana: "Aww. My perfect king."

Bolton: "You all better get going. It is time for school."

Hearing Mr. Rabeau, they all hurry to grab their bags and drive off to school.

.......Back in Vandori Woods.......

Salvador: "I cannot believe that idiotic task force found me! I need a new plan and fast. But how?"

He punches the cave wall of his new hideout and sets a new fire. Salvador ponders the details of the battle between his men and the Glassbec Task Force for a moment and recollects seeing a kid running up to his cabin at the corner of his eye.

Salvador: "Wait a minute, there was some kid sneaking up on my top three crew members. Of course. It must have been him who ruined my operations."

He thinks of a new plan in his head by marking the same break-in maps his associates Marino, Kumal, and Mitchell used before they were imprisoned.

Salvador: "Oh yes, there will be no way that Captain Riles will interfere this time. I might even become a rich man by nightfall. Hahahahaha!"

He grabs a pistol and jumps into an old clunker car.

Salvador: "Time to hot wire this bad boy. We are in business."

.......30 minutes later.......

Salvador drives into Glassbec and decides to park at the side of a gas station sitting a couple of blocks away from the main headquarters of Glassbec's Task Force.

Salvador: "Okay, time to make an entrance."

He kicks in the door and shoots all three cameras and two alarms out with no issue.

Salvador: "All right everyone, don't move and put your paws and hooves up now!"

Rabbit Store Clerk: "Please do not hurt anyone! I will give you all the money you want!"

The store clerk puts all the money from the register on the counter.

Salvador: "Oh, you see that! Someone is getting with the program. Keep it coming rabbit clerk! Now, I want every furry who is here on the floor now."

Female Deer Furry: "Okay."

Little Fawn Furry: "Momma, I am scared!"

Female Deer Furry: "It is going to be okay, Darius. Stay close."

Salvador: "Lady! Tell the kid to keep his yap shut or I will do it for him!"

Female Deer Furry: "Leave him alone, he's just a child!"

Salvador: "No one tells me what to do! I am the one in charge here!"

Salvador bashes her head against the counter. Darius cries out and tries helping her up, but is grabbed by Salvador, holding a knife to his neck.

Salvador: "Listen kid, if you wanna survive this then you and the clerk girl here will do exactly what I say. Get the picture? Good, cause you're now a part of my plan to get some payback."

Darius: "You are mean. Why are you doing this?"

Salvador: "You call it mean. I call it settling scores, kid. Now go with the clerk and get on your knees!"

Darius: "Fine!"

Salvador: "What did you say?"

Darius: "Nothing."

Salvador: "That's what I thought."

Salvador turns the lights off in the convenience store and ties up Darius and his mother while the store clerk cowers behind the register. Afterwards, he makes a call to an old associate.

Salvador: "Hey Damon, I got a job for you."

Damon: "It's been a while since I have completed a job for you. What is the score?"

Salvador: "Just kidnap this rabbit girl from Wild Eye High School."

Damon: "Hehehe. What does she look like?"

Salvador: "Should be a slim one with brown fur and blue eyes. She should also be seen with a dhole named Jackson something or other."

Damon: "Send me a photo. She is one of those rich kids, right?"

Salvador: "That is correct. We are gonna be rich after a nice hefty ransom from her family."

Damon: "Count me in."

.......40 minutes later.......

Damon: "Let's see, where would I find a dhole furry with a rabbit furry?"

Jackson: "How do proms typically go on in this new world?"

Taciana: "Jackson, are you saying that you have never been to a prom?"

Jackson: "Well to be honest, I kinda just thought that it was a stale event with people dancing in some kinda trance after drinking."

Taciana: "Hehe, I used to think that when I was dating Chuvo Ramos."

Jackson: "What happened?"

Taciana: "He got drunk a lot after trying out this new form of wine called Grassy Daze. We never got to dance once because he kept drinking. That is why I dumped him."

Jackson: "Is he still an alcoholic?"

Taciana: "Not as much anymore, but he still drinks after school ends."

Jackson: "Well I hope he gets that issue under control at some point."

Taciana: "Yeah, totally."

They continue talking by Jackson's car after the other Rabeau siblings walk into the school building. Damon creeps in closer by staying low behind the other vehicles in the parking lot. He aims his Glock-50 pistol at them both.

Damon: "Do not even think of moving an inch or I will blow your brains all over this hot rod. Capiche?"

Jackson: "We get the point man. What do you want from us?"

Damon: "I was hired to do a job, not ask questions. Keep your eyes closed while I tie you both up."

He aims his gun at Taciana's back and binds both of her paws.

Jackson: "Aim that at me, you ginormous jerk."

Damon: "Killing you both would be fun, but Salvador has other plans."

Taciana: "Let us go!"

Jackson: "Don't you dare touch her!"

Damon: "Who is going to make me?"

Damon then forces them to cross the street and into his stolen car. Jackson comforts Taciana during the drive as they are taken to the captured gas station.

Jackson: "I will get us out of this. You will see once he and his so-called partner turn their backs."

Taciana: "Okay, I trust you."

Jackson: "That's the spirit."

.......20 minutes later.......

Damon: "Alright, get in the store immediately!"

Jackson and Taciana are placed with the other hostages by Damon.

Salvador: "It is good to see you again, partner."

Damon: "Likewise. So, what is this plan of yours, old friend?"

As the two bear furries converse about Salvador's plan outside the store; Jackson cautiously slides a piece of broken glass from one of the video cameras towards him with his left foot. He carefully cuts off his restraints and then releases Taciana from hers as well.

Rabbit Store Clerk: "What are you doing?"

Jackson: "I am going to cut us all loose and find a way out of here."

Darius: "Mister? Is my Momma going to be okay?"

Jackson: "I will make sure of it."

Taciana: "Hey, be careful!"

Jackson: "Always."

Jackson crouches and hides behind one of the aisles at the back of the store.

Salvador: "Damon? Where is the dhole?"

Damon: "He was right there by the register with restraints on his wrists."

Salvador roars and smashes the display up front and grabs his pistol. Damon and Salvador begin searching around for any sign of Jackson.

Salvador: "Find him! Come on out, Jackson!"

Damon: "Look, all we want is the money from your girl's family! Surrender yourself or we start executing hostages!"

Jackson throws a liquor bottle at a freezer to distract them.

Salvador: "I will search over there, while you keep your eye on our four captives."

Damon: "Got it."

Jackson then stabs Salvador twice in the arm and his leg with a screwdriver he picked off the shelf. Salvador attempts to grab him while trying to reach for his gun. Jackson then kicks him in the head while he is down.

Salvador: "Gaaah! Why you little sneak!"

Jackson: "I already called the Task Force and they are on their way right now."

Salvador: "Damon! Shoot this overconfident fool!"

Damon: "Hahaha, with pleasure."

Jackson: "How about a new deal, Salvador. You and your cohort can be taken out by me and the Task Force or you can live and let all five of us go."

Salvador: "That is not much of a deal for me and my partner over there."

Jackson: "Captain Riles texted me saying that my family is very worried about me and Taciana."

Salvador: "I am not going to surrender to a teenage dhole."

Jackson sticks his third paw nail in Salvador's open cut to make him reconsider his offer. Taciana then pulls Damon's knife out of his holster and stabs him in the torso.

Salvador: "Owwww! You are freaking crazy, kid!"

Damon: "Ahhh shoot! Now you are going to pay!"

Jackson: "No!"

He runs to Taciana's aid and kicks their wounded kidnapper, causing him to fall to the ground. Then the doors burst open with Task Force members aiming at Damon, with Quentin at the lead.

Quentin: "Freeze! Stay on the ground, dirt bag!"

Damon: "I ain't going to prison!"

He lifts his paw and fires one off at Ramirez's chest.

Quentin: "Hands behind your back!"

He handcuffs Damon and hands him to Viscalli for booking. Viscalli puts in the back of the squad van and orders two Task Force members to watch him.

Viscalli: "I am assuming your friend Salvador is in here too, huh?"

Damon: "What's it to you?"

Quentin: "Are you all alright?"

Jackson: "Yes, sir."

Taciana: "The other one named Damon, he held us at gunpoint and tried to use us as ransom."

Quentin: "Okay, just wait with Ramirez and Viscalli. I already told one of them to take you two to school."

Jackson: "What about Darius? His mother needs medical attention."

Quentin: "We already got that covered. Our medical teams have already arranged a transport for her and her child to Saint Glassbec Hospital."

Jackson: "Thank you. I am just glad it is over, Captain."

Quentin: "I think we should be the ones thanking you, son. You helped us catch the last two members of the Clawtooth Clan."

Taciana: "You truly are the Glassbec Hero."

Darius: "He knocked the bad men down!"

Taciana: "He sure did. How about we go check on your Momma, okay?"

Darius: "Yeah!"

Female Deer Furry: "What happened?"

Darius: "Momma!"

Female Deer Furry: "I am still here, baby."

Darius: "The bad men tried to hurt us but Mr. Jackson stopped them."

Female Deer Furry: "That is good news, sweetie. Thank you for your help and for saving my little boy."

Jackson: "Not a problem, miss."

Female Deer Furry: "You can call me Varia. Varia Tuppleson."

Jackson: "It's nice to meet you, Ms. Tuppleson."

Varia: "Varia is fine, Jackson."

Jackson: "You know if you want to talk or grab a drink together, just give me a call."

Varia: "You like coffee?"

Jackson: "Depends on the type."

Varia: "I can make us both a cappuccino or maybe some hot chocolate."

Jackson: "Make it hot chocolate and you got a deal, Varia."

Varia: "Cool. I will see you then, Jackson Tontione."

Darius: "Why did you wink at him, Momma?"

Varia: "It is an adult thing, sweetie."

Darius: "Are you and Mr. Jackson friends now?"

Varia: "Yes, Mr. Jackson and I are friends."

She then carries Darius out of the store and waits for the hospital truck to pick them up.

Store Clerk: "I know I am just a part-time store clerk, but I recognize you from our school."

Jackson: "I have never seen you at school or anywhere for that matter."

Rabbit Store Clerk: "Well, my name is Daisy Sommers."

Jackson: "Call me Jackson Le Tontione or J.T. for short."

Daisy: "Okay and got it. I will see you later at school, Hero of Glassbec."

Jackson: "Sure. If you wanna hang with me and my friends, then yeah."

Daisy: "Splendid!"

She goes outside to give a statement to one of the Task Force operatives.

Jackson: "Surprises around every corner."

.......25 minutes later.......

The pair are finally driven back to the school parking lot by Viscalli.

Viscalli: "Good luck kids!"

Jackson: "I guess we should probably go to class."

Taciana: "Actually Jacky, we do not have to go in at all."

Jackson: "What do you mean?"

Taciana: "Thanks to me, we now have three days off due to our recent and life-threatening situation."

Jackson: "How did you manage that?"

Taciana: "I texted the principal about it and he let all of our teachers know as well.

Jackson: "I gotta tell you Tacci, what you did back there was very brave too."

Taciana: "Hehehe, you inspired me to fight for what is right, hun. Could you maybe teach me some of your fighting styles someday?"

Jackson: "Perhaps."

Taciana: "I would love to learn more about them. Turn on some tunes! Hehe!"

Jackson: "Rock and Roll!"

Jackson flips the radio on and as he and Taciana swiftly zoom out of the parking lot and return home.

Days of Fame and Pleasure

Taciana's parents rush to her with concern as she pulls into the driveway.

Saba: "Taciana! Jackson! Are you alright? What happened?"

Jackson: "We were ambushed by one of Salvador's old friends and the two brutes attempted to use us as leverage."

Bolton: "You mean the maniac who believes that all furries should show allegiance by following him into a life of crime?"

Taciana: "Yes, and only one canine could truly stop them."

Bolton: "You mean Quentin Riles from the town's task force? He's the one who called us after he said one of you texted him for help."

Taciana: "I meant Jackson, Daddy."

Saba: "Would that explain why your sisters ran inside the house without saying a word for almost seven days?"

Taciana: "Yes."

Bolton: "You did protect my Taciana and even risked your life doing so. From now on son, you are an honorary member of this family."

Jackson: "Thank you, sir."

Bolton: "Go on your two. Enjoy the rest of your day off."

Saba: "You think they will be okay by themselves, honey bun?"

Bolton: "Those two are going to be just fine."

Saba: "I need reassurance of my children's safety, Bolton! I don't want to hear about anymore abductions, especially if it involves one of our own."

Bolton: "If it makes you feel better, I will hire a security guard to watch the mansion while we are at work."

Saba: "Thank you."

The two head off to work to run their multi-billiondollar company, Rabeau Incorporated.

Taciana: "Now that the parents are gone and there aren't many assignments left for the remainder of the quarter, I think we deserve a little downtime."

Jackson: "I would think so, considering the day we had."

Taciana: "Hehe, well we could both be international heroes."

Jackson: "Haha, I could see the headlines now; daring duo disrupts a bank robbery and jails the criminals."

Taciana: "Would I really make a great heroine?"

Jackson: "Why do you ask that?"

Taciana: "I mean, you were the one that actually took those two down and I just cowered a little and saw an opportunity to strike. It is not the hero thing to do."

Jackson: "Hey come on, there is nothing you should be ashamed of, babe. If you didn't distract that big brute, I wouldn't be here right now. Besides, you are my special heroine."

Taciana: "Hehe, you do have a way with words. How was I so lucky to find someone like you?"

Jackson: "I am your gift from the stars, am I not?"

They have a quick healthy dinner before walking into the main TV room. The two finish off their day together by watching the sports channel, FSTN, Furry Sports Television Network.

Taciana: "Who do you think is going to win? I am hedging my bets on the team with the blue uniforms."

Jackson: "Babe, it is more about the skill of the individuals on the team than the color of their uniforms."

Taciana: "I haven't ever been much of a sports fan so I wouldn't know."

Jackson: "I'll teach you about it during college."

Taciana: "Really?"

Jackson: "Sure, I can do that and give you some pointers about basketball, soccer, football, baseball, and maybe even tennis."

Taciana: "You teaching me something?"

Jackson: "Yeah, it will be like reversing roles for a day or two, baby."

Taciana: "I will consider it; if you do something for me on that day."

Jackson: "What would that be, Tacci?"

Taciana: "You have to take me to a fancy restaurant called the Moroccan Club."

Jackson: "How about this for a deal? If the Glassbec Gryphons win, then I choose the restaurant."

Taciana: "Okay, if that team wins you choose the restaurant and you get to teach me about every sport you know."

Jackson: "It's a deal."

.......The Second Day Off.......

The next day Jackson is called by the Worldwide Furry Network for a live interview at 8:00 in the morning. Jackson and Taciana drive to the Worldwide Furry TV Station.

Taciana: "You can do this, Jacky. Plus, after what happened yesterday, the principal gave us plenty of time off to recover."

Jackson: "It is not a problem for me but I haven't been on a live telecast before. Am I getting too nervous?"

Taciana: "You shouldn't be, baby. Not to mention the prom is this Friday and with you at my side we could end up becoming the new king and queen of the party."

She adjusts his necktie and tells him to take a breath before walking out in front of the camera.

Jackson: "Alright I can do this."

Jimmy Findello: "There he is ladies and gentlemen, the man of the hour, Jackson Le Tontione!"

Jackson waves his paw to the camera and takes a seat in the chair.

Jimmy Findello: "Jackson, all of our viewers want to know how it feels to face off against Glassbec's most wanted."

Jackson: "To be honest, Mr. Findello, it felt like it was going to be my last moment alive and I was afraid of losing the girl I love to Salvador and his accomplice."

Jimmy: "So, you have a special lady in your life?"

Jackson: "Yes I do. She has always been there for me and I would do the same for her. That also includes defending her with my life."

Jimmy: "Have you ever thought of protecting Glassbec and joining the Task Force?"

Jackson: "I have thought about it, but I realize now that it is better to know where you are needed the most."

Jimmy: "I respect that big time!"

Jackson: "Thank you for your understanding, Mr. Findello. It has been an honor to finally be recognized for heroic accolades."

Mr. Findello: "It was great having you with us this afternoon, Mr. Tontione. Have a great day now. There you have it, folks, a local hero and man of his word. Thank you and goodnight!"

Jackson: "What did you think of my performance?"

Taciana: "That was fabulous, darling! You nailed it like a news anchor!"

Jackson: "Plus I kept my statements from getting too personal."

Taciana: "Excellent."

.......1 hour later.......

They go home and tell Mr. and Mrs. Rabeau about their day when they came back from work. Finally, the day then ends with Jackson and Taciana going to bed.

.......The Third Day Off.......

Taciana: "I am not feeling so good sugar, would you be a darling and bring me some herbal tea and Vitamin C, please?"

Jackson: "Sure thing, hun."

As he goes down the stairs some of the other girls from school call, asking him out to the prom after watching the news report. He declines them all since his decision has already been made with his divine looking girlfriend. He brings the medicine and lemon tea for Taciana and tells her that he'll be back with a surprise for her.

.......50 minutes later.......

He purchases a black streamlined tux with red tie at Raikan's Suits and goes to Valera's Boutique for Taciana's clothes.

Jackson: "Tacci won't be able to take her eyes off me while I am wearing this, and she'll be looking like a dime in this one. Hi there, sweetheart. I'm looking to buy a prom dress for my girlfriend, but I am not sure what to pick. Any ideas?"

Valera Catalani: "We do have options for ladies who need that special touch from their man. Come this way young sir."

The mouse furry shows him her shop's number one prom dresses for sale and Jackson spots the perfect choice.

Jackson: "I choose the one that had lace chiffon on it."

Valera: "You have a good eye, sir. I take it that your lady friend is into exquisite designs."

Jackson: "You have no idea."

Valera: "Come on, I will ring you up."

After Valera scans the tag on the prom dress and places it in one plastic bag, she covers it with another to avoid the risk of tearing.

Valera: "Have a good day, Jackson."

Jackson: "You know me?"

Valera: "Yeah, I know you from history class and I saw the news report about you when I was channel surfing."

Jackson: "Oh okay, thanks."

Jackson: "I'll see you then, Valera."

Valera: "Wow, Riley was right. Seeing a handsome dhole like him can really take a girl's breath away."

.......50 minutes later.......

Jackson drives home and walks back to his cottage where Taciana is on the couch, asleep. He hides his new tux and Taciana's prom dress inside of his bedroom closet.

Jackson: "Wow she is like an angel when she sleeps."

Taciana: "I can still hear you, big man."

Jackson: "Impressive hearing."

Taciana: "I am feeling a lot better now, babe."

Jackson: "I am glad you're feeling like yourself again, my Tacci."

Scoring a Date

The following morning, Taciana wakes up feeling much better and looks around to try cooking something new in the kitchen. She makes an omelette while toasting two slices of bread for Jackson. Then she delivers it to his room in the guest cottage. She opens his bedroom door and places a standing tray over his lap. Jackson yawns as Taciana strokes his short military style hair.

Taciana: "Hey, handsome hero. I brought you breakfast."

Jackson: "Aww, you shouldn't have, babe."

Taciana: "Made your eggs just the way you like them."

Jackson: "Why are you so giddy this early?"

Taciana: "Because tomorrow is prom night and I cannot wait to see what you bought me yesterday."

Jackson: "Okay, but close your eyes."

Taciana: "Oooh, I love a surprise!"

Jackson: "Alright, now you can open them."

Taciana: "Oh wow! A lace chiffon dress with a slit in the front?"

Jackson: "If it is too much then I could take it back."

Taciana: "Are you kidding? I love it! I love it!" Thank you, babe!"

Jackson: "You are welcome, sugar bunny. Don't proms normally have only snacks or hors d'oeuvres?"

Taciana: "Yeah they do, Jacky. However, we are not going to eat at the prom like everyone else. We are going to have an actual pre-made dinner just for us."

Jackson: "For real?"

Taciana: "Yeah, it would be a good starter before we dance the night away at the Emperor Ballroom."

Jackson: "Is that where everyone goes for a general party zone in this town?"

Taciana: "No silly dhole, there is actually a Green Lagoon where we like to go for a swim."

Jackson: "Sounds like a good idea too."

They share a kiss before Warrick walks in on them.

Warrick: "Oh sorry, about that. I will let you carry on with your moment."

Taciana: "Wait, Warrick! What did you want to tell us?"

Warrick: "I actually need your advice on something."

Jackson: "Advice on what?"

Warrick: "Renet has been a little worried about how she will look at the dance."

Jackson: "Try calming her down and tell her that she looks perfectly fine."

Warrick: "You sure that works?"

Jackson: "If it can work on my beautiful Tacci, then it will work on Renet."

Warrick: "Thanks dude. I will talk it over with Renet and help her through her worries after school today."

Taciana: "Go get her, big brother. I cannot have one of my best friends alone for the dance."

Warrick goes down the stairs and dials Renet's number.

Warrick: "Renet."

Renet: "Hey War, what's up?"

Warrick: "Are you feeling alright?"

Renet: "To be honest, Warrick, I am feeling better."

Warrick: "You sure? What changed your mind?"

Renet: "It is going to be the last time we can be the prom queen and king of the year."

Warrick: "Renet, you know that doesn't really matter to me, right?"

Renet: "I figured you would want to win like last year."

Warrick: "All that matters to me is having you by my side."

Renet: "Come over to school and I will give you a surprise."

Warrick: "A surprise?"

Renet: "You are going to have to find out. I love you."

Warrick: "Love you too, Renet."

Renet: "He will be very surprised about this."

She holds a silver watch in her hand and hides it in her pocket.

Warrick: "At least she is not stressed out anymore."

Taciana: "That is a good sign."

The trio eat their breakfast and wake the other three Rabeau sisters, but Ramona refuses to move.

Jackson: "It is time to roll out, Ramona."

Ramona: "Are you going to the prom with me?"

Jackson: "No."

Ramona: "Then I am not moving an inch."

Taciana: "Come on, sis. You still have one day to find a date."

Ramona: "A date with who? Nobody has even bothered to ask me yet!"

Taciana: "That is not true, Ramona. There is still that one guy in our physics class."

Ramona: "You mean Martin Rivera, the coyote?"

Taciana: "Yeah I heard from Sophia that he tried asking her out."

Ramona: "Did she say yes when he did?"

Taciana: "No, he ran away looking super nervous."

Ramona: "Hmm. He did help me complete the online study guide for the final physics exam."

Taciana: "I know how much you like furries who are into the field of science."

Ramona: "Yeah, he is a brainiac, isn't he? You are right, it's time to move on."

Taciana: "That's the spirit, little sister!"

Jackson: "No hard feelings, right?"

Ramona: "Of course, Jackson. If you two are happy together, then I'm happy."

Taciana: "Thanks, sis."

Warrick: "Great to see you two getting along again, but my girl is waiting for me."

Jackson: "He is right, ladies. We need to get to school early."

.......25 minutes later.......

Jackson and the Rabeaus drive into the parking lot and see all of their friends at the front of the school.

Natasha: "Hey look, it's Jackson!"

Carina: "I am going to ask him first."

Natasha: "Not if I get to him first."

Amber: "I am the one who is going with him!"

Nova: "No me!"

Melody: "Slim chance, sister!"

Gulani: "Obviously he is mine."

Pepper: "He is going to be my date!"

Ava: "Jackson deserves someone loyal like me!"

Sophia: "You all are nuts if you think anyone here will get my Jackson!"

Riley: "Could you all stop arguing for one morning?"

Natasha: "What are you talking about, Riley? You were after him too."

Riley: "Miles already asked me and I said yes to his offer."

Abby: "That is great, Riley! I knew you would get lucky before the dance."

Evelyn: "You kept trying and that is what counts."

Renet goes up to Warrick as he and the others approach the sidewalk.

Renet: "Hi, War."

Warrick: "Hey, babe."

Renet: "Here is your surprise."

She gives him the silver watch and wraps it around his wrist.

Warrick: "Nice, now I can look like a working man."

Renet: "Hehehe. My grateful rabbit man."

Warrick: "I am glad I met you when I did."

Renet: "You mean during freshman year by the lockers?"

.......Flashback to 5016.......

Warrick: "Another day in paradise."

Renet: "I do not care if you are the principal's assistant, Vince!"

Vince: "The principal is hardly ever in his office."

Renet: "Get your paws off me!"

Vince: "Feisty as always, rabbit.

Warrick: "Yo Vinny! Let the little lady go."

Vince: "Haha, you better keep walking Warrick, I already busted you up before."

Warrick jumps, kicks Vince's back leg, and smacks him to the ground.

Renet: "Is he still conscious?"

Warrick: "Nah, he is out cold."

Renet: "Appreciate the backup."

Warrick: "No need to thank me, sweet eyes."

Renet: "Vince has always been a real prick for a common cat. May I ask your name?"

Warrick: "Warrick Rabeau."

Renet: "You mean like Rabeau Industries?"

Warrick: "That is correct, my parents run the show over there."

Renet: "I am Renet Taylor."

Warrick: "Are you a Gryphon's fan?"

Renet: "Sure am."

Warrick: "Do you want to go out for ice cream or something?"

Renet: "Ice cream does sound good."

Warrick: "Cool, I am buying."

Renet: "No, no. I can pay for our dessert. It's not a problem."

Warrick: "You sure?"

Renet: "Warrick, you rescued me even though we had just met. That speaks a good volume about you in my book. Let's go, War."

Warrick: "War?"

Renet: "It is your new nickname, silly."

Warrick: "I might get used to that."

The two walk out his truck and drive to the plaza near the center of town.

.......Present Day 5020.......

Renet: "Hehe, I called you War for the first time on that late afternoon."

Warrick: "Mmmmwah."

Renet: "Mmmmwah."

The two then follow everyone else into the building after reminiscing about that fortuitous day.

.......During Lunchtime.......

Ramona: "Did all of them stop arguing over Jackson, yet?"

Taciana: "Nope, as far I can tell Carina, Natasha, Nova, and Melody are still at each other's throats over who gets to be with him for the prom dance."

Ramona: "I guess they still need time to get past the whole obsession thing, like me."

Taciana: "Yeah, I suppose so. I am just glad that some of the other girls stopped making moves on him."

Ramona: "What are you saying?"

Taciana: "I am saying that every girl who hasn't gotten a date is always staring at him like he's a prize, especially after that news video of him went viral."

Ramona: "Speaking of finding a date, I am off to nail one. Catch you at the lunchroom, Tacci."

Martin: "One more physics course to ace and I shall be the molecular physicist of the future!"

Ramona: "Hi Martin."

Martin: "Hi Ramona."

Ramona: "I know this is surprising; but would like to go to the prom with me tomorrow?"

Martin: "Sure, I'll take you there."

Ramona: "You will?"

Martin: "Yeah."

Ramona: "Yes!"

Martin: "It is mainly because I am the most clever student in the school, correct?"

Ramona: "There is that, and I kinda have a thing for furry boys with impressive intelligence."

Martin: "Are you serious?"

Ramona: "Pick me up at 7:00 pm tomorrow, future physicist. See you later."

Martin: "I got a date. Huh? What are the odds?"

Jackson: "Here is my autograph."

Female Fennec Fox Furry: "Oh yay! Thank you, Hero of Glassbec!"

Jackson: "Nice to meet a fan."

Female Fennec Fox Furry: "My name is Kona."

Jackson: "Nice to meet you."

Kona: "Likewise. How did you take down two bear furries single handedly?"

Jackson: "Follow me to lunch and I will explain everything."

.......3 hours and 48 minutes later.......

Taciana: "I have to ask you something, Jacky."

Jackson: "What is it,Tacci?"

Taciana: "Who was the new girl you were talking to?"

Jackson: "Her name is Kona and she is a fan of the Hero of Glassbec."

Taciana: "Hmph."

Jackson: "Relax, bunny boo, she is only a fan and nothing more."

Taciana: "Well, alright."

Jackson: "We are definitely going to need plenty of sleep before the dance."

Taciana: "True, but we are going to practice a popular style of dance called the Samba once we return home."

Jackson: "Then you are leading the way on that one, babe."

Taciana: "Trust me, I will be."

Dance Practice

Jackson and Taciana walk through the mansion's front door holding paws, only to notice Bolton and Saba having a toast at the kitchen table.

Bolton: "You know dear, I think we should take the week off from the company and have a little "us" time."

Saba: "Hehehe, cheers. Hey kids, how was school?"

Jackson: "It went better than expected, Mrs. Rabeau."

Saba: "Why is that, Jackson?"

Jackson: "I was asked out by tons of furry girls."

Taciana: "Ahem!"

Jackson: "However, I declined because I already have my dream girl right here."

Taciana: "This primo furry thought it would be better to ask me to the prom at the lunchroom in front of everyone!"

Jackson: "You were so red."

Taciana: "Needless to say, I was very impressed."

.......10 minutes later.......

Ramona, Tawny, Serena, come in tout suite and get their prom clothes ready for tomorrow.

Ramona: "This color is so me. Hopefully Martin will ask me to dance with him before I ask him. Sigh. Get it together, girl, he is your new knight in shining armor and you will have a good time."

Serena: "Oh my gosh, calm down sister."

Ramona: "How can I be calm? I don't even know if he likes me or not."

Serena: "Mona, relax. I'm sure Martin does."

Ramona: "How do you know?"

Serena: "I sat behind him a few times in class and I believe I overheard him say that you have an exceptional mind."

Ramona: "He really said that?"

Serena: "Yup."

Tawny: "You shouldn't even be worrying, Ramona. We are the ones who are going stag along with everyone else."

Ramona: "Thanks. I didn't think you two would support me in this matter."

Serena: "Please sis, we all know how important tomorrow is to you."

.......15 minutes later.......

Jackson: "So, you are a highly proficient dancer of the Samba?"

Taciana: "Darling, the two of us will have this routine down easily."

Jackson: "Uhm, I've changed my mind. Let us try something else.

Taciana: "Don't be nervous, my bae. We are going to ace La Samba tonight!"

Jackson: "Okay honey, I believe you."

Jackson turns on his music speaker and makes a special request for the practice run.

Jackson: "Orvune, play Baila al Ritmo for us."

Speaker: "Playing Baila al Ritmo."

Taciana: "Do you know what that means, bae?"

Jackson: "No, what does it mean?"

Taciana: "Hehehe, it means dance to the beat."

Jackson: "You can speak Spanish too?"

Taciana: "Si, seguro que puedo." (Yes, I sure can.)

Jackson: "Truly impressive."

Taciana: "You bet."

.......Several hours later.......

Taciana: "Will you catch me in the air after our dance is complete?"

Jackson: "No worries, my delicate rose, I'd be ready for you anytime."

After giving her his promise she smiles and backs up to run at him at 37 miles per hour.

Jackson: "I gotcha, Tacci."

Taciana: "Yeah! You really caught me."

Jackson: "Told you."

He sets her down as she embraces his neck and stares into his eyes.

Taciana: "Hmm, I guess that is enough practice for tonight."

Jackson: "Remember that other promise you made me keep?"

Taciana: "The one which involved you singing to me?"

Jackson: "Yup."

Taciana: "I never forgot that, honey."

Jackson: "Okay, fasten your seatbelt."

Jackson starts singing to her using his tenor voice.

.......Jackson's Song.......

"Many years, I searched for a calling,

This is all for you and me,

In all of that time alone,

I knew something was bound to happen,

Now I see that you were meant to be for me,

Staring right at me with great curiosity,

Right then and there I knew well,

That you were meant for me,

Under the brightness of the moon,

You defended me like I belong here,

I can't express how grateful I am,

You have the courage of many,

Haters try to stop my progress,

Don't ever give up on anything,

We stand stronger if united as one,

We chase the solution for peace,

Standing in another's shoes,

Yet we belong eternally

In a land changed for the better,

When will we be seen as one?"

.......End of Jackson's Song.......

Taciana: "Oh Jacky, that was beautiful. What is the name of the song?"

Jackson: "I call it A Sense of Belonging."

Taciana: "Inspiring."

Bolton and Saba stood outside of Jackson's room tapping their feet.

Jackson: "Oh, hey Mr. and Mrs. Rabeau!"

Taciana: "Hi Daddy."

Bolton: "It is very late and you two should be asleep already!"

Saba: "Hun, we talked about being gentle with them before, remember?"

Bolton: "Alright! Alright! Could you two turn off the music and go to sleep, please?"

Jackson: "Not a problem, sir. We were feeling pretty tired anyways. Right, babe?"

Taciana: "Absolutely."

Bolton: "Okay then, goodnight."

Taciana's parents leave the room.

Saba: "You need to be a little gentle when dealing with Taciana and Jackson. I trust Jackson to treat our daughter with respect and make her happy."

Bolton: "Saba, this is our eldest daughter we are talking out."

Saba: "I think he is good for her, Bolton."

Bolton: "She said the same thing about that Chuvo Ramos she was with a while back."

Saba: "Bolton, she wanted to break up with him because you said you hated how he drinks beer and wine every day. It would be nice if you actually accepted Jackson as part of this family."

Bolton: "Fine, I will accept him as my future son-in-law."

Saba: "I want you to tell him that."

Bolton reopens the door to Jackson's room and tells him that he would be more than glad to have him as his son-in-law.

Jackson: "I won't let you down, sir. I mean, Dad."

Bolton: "Marry my daughter first and then you can call me that."

Taciana: "He will get used to you, bae. You just need to schedule some macho bonding time."

Jackson: "You mean like going on a guy's trip."

Taciana: "Yes, exactly."

Jackson: "I am willing to give it a shot if he is."

Taciana: "I will convince him one day.

Jackson: "If you say so, sugar bunny."

Prom Night

The day of the prom arrives with Taciana's blue eyes opening up to the sun shining down on her face. She skips over to the guest cottage where Jackson is still sleeping. As she pokes him, Jackson groans and continues sleeping.

Taciana: "Jackson? It is time for my hero to wake up. Okay then, time for my secret weapon."

She sprays peach scented perfume all over herself, making Jackson's sensitive canine nose go crazy.

Taciana: "Now for my lipstick."

Jackson: "Wow, something smells scrumptious!"

Taciana: "You mean like me?"

Jackson: "You get dressed real fast."

Taciana: "I need to ask if we have our private ride for the prom, Jacky."

Jackson: "Chill, my Tacci, I got this."

He calls up the Glassbec Limo Services for a one-night drive special.

Jackson: "You are coming by the mansion at 8:00 pm? Excellent. Thank you."

Taciana: "We are going to be driven to and from the prom, right?"

Jackson: "Of course we are, my rabbit love. It will all go as planned."

Bolton: "Why did Taciana have to be the one child who wakes earlier than everyone else?"

Saba: "Bolton what is wrong now?"

Bolton: "I cannot wrap my head around the idea of our son and four daughters going away to college. Can't they just stay around for a little longer while attending a local college for a couple more years?"

Saba: "That is a great idea, hun. Our children could attend close to here and then transfer to a big university."

Bolton: "That way we can keep an eye on them."

Saba: "That and tuition is cheaper at a community college. Therefore, saving us plenty of money. I would suggest sending them all to Golden Oak Community College first and they could transfer over to Wood Creek University."

Bolton: "Glad we agree on that, Saba."

Saba grabs the hash browns, fruit, and veggies while Bolton grabs the bacon and bread for Jackson.

.......35 minutes later.......

Saba: "Breakfast is ready!"

Bolton: "Come on down when you are ready kids!"

Saba: "Well good morning lovebirds."

Taciana: "Mom!"

Saba: "Relax, everyone around town is aware of you and Jackson's status, dear."

Taciana: "What does that mean?"

Saba: "It is another way of saying that you claimed Jackson as a mate and you are being very protective of him."

Jackson: "I don't mind if she is, Ms. Rabeau."

Bolton: "Boy, you may want to rethink your answer on that one."

Saba: "Bolton."

Taciana: "You don't mind me being with you most of the time?"

Jackson: "Please, being with you is a drip of fresh water."

.......40 minutes later.......

Taciana: "Let us get going, hun. We have some VIP tickets to pay for once lunchtime comes."

Jackson: "Sounds swell, I cannot wait to live it up like a VIP."

The others followed. Ten minutes later they all arrive at school.

.......Meanwhile at Wild Eye High.......

Ava: "I am telling you, Shauna, Jackson is the only one I can think about."

Shauna: "Then try finding another male furry who can make your dreams come true."

Ava: "That is easy for you to say, Shauna. You have Geoffrey. I am still alone, and no one ever bothered to ask me!"

Shauna: "Hey come on, Ava, cheer up. At least you still have a chance with any guy you come across."

Ava: "It is fine I will go as the only single raccoon girl and buy my ticket."

Ava waits in line to buy her ticket for prom when she sees a few others including some of her friends buying VIP tickets.

Ava: "Might as well go big or go home."

Weldsman: "One VIP ticket to prom?"

Ava: "Yep. Hey everyone, this is Shauna and Geoffrey."

Shauna: "Hi everyone, it is nice to feel included. Right, Geoffrey?"

Geoffrey: "Yup, sure pumpkin."

Shauna: "Geoffrey?"

Geoffrey: "It is nothing to worry about Shauna; I am just inviting my friend over to lunch."

Shauna: "Oh well, that's fine, but don't let him talk about his molecular physics award the whole time he is here."

Ramona: "Molecular physics?"

Geoffrey: "Yeah he is a real scientific expert at it."

Then a familiar coyote comes to the table and Ramona just melts at the sight of him.

Ramona: "Oooh, hi Martin."

Martin: "Good afternoon, Ramona. What's up Geoffrey? You ready for the final's next week?"

Geoffrey: "Heck yeah! But tonight we party like rock stars, bro!"

The two friends give each other high fives.

Ramona: "Shauna, are they always going to be like this?"

Shauna: "Hopefully not."

Geoffrey: "Hey come on ladies, you are staring at a pair of super geniuses."

Shauna: "Geoffrey, you are doing it again."

Ramona: "Don't be ashamed of them Shauna; I think it is nice that they are trying to impress us."

Shauna: "Martin, did you happen to find a corsage for your date?"

Martin: "Yeah, what is that?"

Shauna: "It has always been a custom for the man to put a corsage on his girl. So do you have one?"

Martin then unzips his lucky pack and reaches in revealing a blue corsage. He wraps the corsage around Ramona's wrist. She hugs him.

Martin: "For you, Ramona."

Ramona: "A blue iris? Martin, this is so beautiful!"

Martin: "I didn't know making your girl happy involved being constricted!"

Geoffrey: "Trust me, my friend, Shauna is all over me every time she receives something shiny on her birthday."

Shauna: "What was that, Geoffrey?"

Geoffrey: "Just an inside guy joke, babe."

Shauna: "Okay."

Jackson: "Love is certainly in the air today, huh?"

Tobias: "Whew, tell me about it."

Miles: "I hear you man, but the furry ladies will not stop until they find a mate by any means necessary."

Jackson: "They actually say that in these times?"

Miles: "It is true. For example, Riley was crazy about you and now she is all about staying with me."

Jackson: "Is that why most of the girls in our merry band have been hitting on me?"

Yahar: "They are right, bro. Evelyn couldn't keep her paws off me when I won her a prize at the spring fair last year."

.......Flash back to 5019.......

Evelyn is at the concession stand eating kettle corn and noticed a honey badger with sick skills at a bottle hitting contest.

Evelyn: "I want to give it a try."

Yahar: "Go ahead."

Evelyn: "Here we go."

She throws the ball three times but only hits half of the bottles.

Evelyn: "This is so hard!"

Yahar: "May I?"

He places his own quarter down and throws the ball once, watching as it knocks all the bottles down.

Game Concession Furry: "We have a winner!"

Yahar: "I believe this teddy bear is yours."

Evelyn: "Thank you. What is your name?"

Yahar: "My name is Yahar."

Evelyn: "Evelyn."

Yahar: "Want to explore a little?"

Evelyn: "Hehe, okay. Mind if I hold your arm for a bit?"

Yahar: "Not at all. Why?"

Evelyn: "Cause I want to."

…….Present Day 5020 at 12:00pm…….

Tobias: "So that is why she chose you?"

Yahar: "Well yeah. Evelyn is my badger queen, while I am her aggressive king. How are things with you and Abby, if you don't mind my asking?"

Tobias: "Abby and I are good actually. We even studied all of our class subjects thoroughly last week."

Miles: "You two are prepared for the finals already? Dang! I may have to convince Riley to do the same with me."

Tobias: "What about you, Jackson? Do you and Taciana study together?"

Jackson: "Sometimes we do, but not always."

Tobias: "What happens during the times you don't study."

Jackson: "Taciana wants to talk about her day in class and I talk about my day in class. You know, usual everyday stuff."

.......Meanwhile in the Lunch Line.......

Taciana: "Are you serious? Martin gave you the corsage this early?"

Ramona: "Yes and it was adorable. The way he did it just felt so natural."

Abby: "My Toby plans on driving me to the Emperor Ballroom."

Evelyn: "I'm hoping that Yahar doesn't do his freestyle."

Riley: "Evelyn, a lot of us are going to dance in freestyle to the faster songs."

Evelyn: "Believe me, you don't want to see how he dances to fast beats."

Taciana: "Well, I know Jackson will never want to lead in a new form of dance."

Evelyn: "Really?"

Taciana: "Oh yes, he insisted on me taking the lead."

They all sit and eat together for the rest of lunch and purchase up the remaining VIP tickets afterwards.

.......3 hours and 18 minutes later.......

Afternoon approached as all the students of Wild Eye High left home to prepare themselves for the party.

.......At the Rabeau Mansion.......

Saba: "Bolton. Honey!"

Bolton: "Yeah?"

Saba: "The kids are back. Could you open the door for them, please? I am about to wash my hair."

Bolton: "But the game is nearly over."

Saba: "They have their hands full, Bolton."

Bolton: "We could hire a butler, you know."

Saba: "Bolton!"

Bolton: "Okay, okay I will open the door. Sheesh."

Jackson: "Did you really need to buy all of that make up?"

Taciana: "Yes, because it is part of the surprise I have for you once I am done changing."

Jackson: "This means I have to wait patiently for it, right?"

Taciana: "Hey, don't be pouty. Good things will come, you just need to wait."

She heads up to her room to put on the lace chiffon dress and applies the makeup she bought on her eyes.

Taciana: "Perfect. Time to teach them how to boogie."

Jackson: "The best parts always involve waiting."

.......30 minutes later.......

Jackson quickly changes into his tuxedo and tightens his belt around his pants.

After that he pops in a breath mint before knocking on Taciana's bedroom door.

Jackson: "Hey Tacci, are you done?"

Taciana: "Just a minute! Okay! Come on in."

Jackson opens the door, and his jaw drops before howling with joy.

Taciana: "Such a howler."

Jackson: "Tacania Rabeau, you are a radiant gem."

Taciana: "Hehe, you are quite a snappy dresser yourself, Jackson Le Tontione. Time to roll, we have a limo that awaits us."

Jackson: "I could get used to this."

Taciana nuzzles her nose against his lovingly before he opens the limo's back door for her.

Taciana: "Such a gentleman."

Jackson: "You will be even more impressed with the moves I've mastered."

.......7:00 pm the Rabeau's Mansion.......

Martin: "You got this man. You got this."

He knocks on the big doors and is greeted by Mr. Rabeau.

Bolton: "Yes?"

Martin: "Good afternoon, Mr. Rabeau. I was wondering if Ramona was still here?"

Bolton: "Ramona! There is a stranger at the door who seems to know you."

Ramona: "Daddy, he is not a stranger, he is my date. Come on Martin, we are going to be late and miss the first song."

Bolton: "Have fun, Ramona! Martin, I know where you live."

Martin: "Great meeting you."

.......Meanwhile at the Ballroom at 7:30pm.......

Jackson: "So anyways, that is why my brother Cole called me the Speed King, I always beat everyone who challenged me to a race on the track team."

Taciana: "Whoa, that must have been a hard part of your life maintaining such a title."

Jackson: "Nah, it wasn't so bad. I did earn first place for three years in a row before the war started."

Taciana: "Do you miss it? Your old life?"

Jackson: "There are days when I reminisce about my former life, but I have moved forward with you and your family."

He reaches across the table and holds her paws for a few more minutes and stares into his girlfriend's eyes. One of the doors opens with many furries including the deejay setting up shop in the main room.

Jackson: "Why did you bring us here early if the party starts at eight?"

Taciana: "So we could bond a little more and learn about each other."

Jackson: "Hehe, I guess it was a good idea for the driver to bring us here early. After all, I did get to know another side of you too."

Taciana: "Our friends should be here at 8:00 pm which is 22 minutes away."

Jackson: "I almost forgot to give you your corsage."

Taciana: "Aww, Jackson, this is amazing. It matches well with my dress."

.......24 minutes later.......

Martin: "Thank you little lady for riding Martin's Python."

Ramona: "Hehehehe. Did you just make that up for my sake?"

Martin: "Oh no Ramona, this is the 5012 Python Rollmaster. My Dad bought it for me since it was my dream car."

Ramona: "You are so lucky. My parents never really buy cars for me or my other siblings."

Martin: "Why?"

Ramona: "They are afraid of us breaking it. So it wouldn't affect their finances, instead they gave us an equal piece of the inheritance to keep us going for many years."

Martin: "Your parents think you're not capable of making the decision to buy a car?"

Ramona: "They only think my sister Taciana and my older brother Warrick are responsible enough to have a vehicle."

Martin: "I think you are a responsible type."

Ramona: "You do?"

Martin: "I think you are responsible enough to do anything."

Ramona: "Could you help me pick out a new car next week?"

Martin: "I may have the physics final next week, but yes, I will fit into my schedule, Mona."

Ramona leans over and presses her lips against his passionately.

Ramona: "Time to have some fun!"

Martin: "Sure, let me just lock the van. Here we go."

Ramona: "Hi Taciana. Nice choice in silk."

Taciana: "Thanks, Ramona."

As they continue talking about different types of fabric, Jackson and Martin talk about the latest basketball game between the Gryphons and the Knights teams.

.......40 minutes later.......

The building is flooded with furries of all kinds from Wild Eye High and they walk towards the main room as the Deejay makes his announcement to the crowd.

Deejay Fury Thunder: "Alright is everyone feeling good tonight?"

Crowd: "Yeah!"

Deejay Fury Thunder: "Time to start things slow. So grab that special someone or find a partner, because it is going to get crazy afterwards!"

The music starts as every furry dances to the slow symphony of a song known as Forever Through the Light. During the song, the group finds their own spot in the crowd to dance and sway to the harmonic beats.

Tobias: "I assume that you're enjoying yourself, my squirrelly love?"

Abby: "I sure am, Toby."

Riley: "Mind if we take this thing we have between us a little further?"

Miles: "I thought you only wanted to dance for the night?

Riley: "I had second thoughts."

Miles: "I take it that this means you have let go of your obsession with Jackson?"

Riley: "Yes, Miles Booker, that is what this means."

Miles: "What type of dance were you thinking of for the next song?"

Riley: "How about we try it in freestyle."

Miles: "Works for me."

.......3 hours of dancing later.......

Deejay Fury Thunder: "Alright everybody listen up, this is the last song of the evening, The Dream of Your Eyes! However, this will only involve the two who win the contest for prom king and queen. Their names are Jackson Le Tontione and Taciana Rabeau! Show them some love folks!"

Crowd: "Woooh!"

Jackson and Taciana stand as one in the middle of the dance floor to perform their Samba routine together for everyone to see.

Taciana: "You sure you are ready?"

Jackson: "Trust me on this."

Amber: "I can't believe it."

Evelyn: "What can't you believe, Amber?"

Amber: "I can't believe someone as handsome as Jackson isn't with me."

Evelyn: "Be happy you had a good time, Amber. I mean it's prom, not a big celebration."

Amber: "I am still not giving up on my desire for that attractive dhole."

Evelyn: "Whatever, you say."

Yahar: "Evelyn, it is almost past twelve in the morning."

Evelyn: "At least stay for the final dance Yahar, they are our friends."

Yahar: "Okay, but all of our parents won't like it."

Ava watches the whole performance unfold with her eyes fixed on Jackson.

Ava: "So majestic."

.......12 minutes later.......

The Samba dance finally ends with Jackson lifting Taciana in the air and setting her down with grace and ease.

Taciana: "We won, baby! We won!"

Jackson: "What did I tell ya?"

She wraps her arms around him as they hug it out and share a kiss under the spotlight.

Crowd: "Awww."

Taciana: "Jacky, they are still watching us."

Jackson: "Don't mind them, my gorgeous bunny. What matters now is you and me."

Final Days of Being Wild

The nightly hours continue with our favorite couple still holding each other in the main room.

Jackson: "Sugar bae, it is already past 2:00 am. We have to go back."

Taciana: "Can't we stay like this for a few more minutes, baby?"

Jackson: "Okay, but only because those eyes are so cute."

Taciana: "Thanks, honey."

After ten more minutes of grooving to the music; Jackson and Taciana walk back to the limo.

Jackson: "Here you are good, sir."

He tips the chauffeur thirty dollars in advance.

Taciana: "Take us home, Mr. Ollister."

Ollister: "You got it."

The rabbit chauffeur starts the limo and drives them back to the Rabeau mansion.

.......45 minutes later.......

Jackson: "Here we are."

Taciana: "Home sweet home."

They hold each other's paws as they reach the front doors and are spotted by Warrick.

Warrick: "I am guessing you two decided to come back, right?"

Jackson: "It is only 2:55 am Warrick."

Warrick: "I gotta say Jackson, you put on quite a show. What is your secret?"

Jackson: "There is no secret about how me and Taciana performed the Samba."

Warrick: "Come on dude, seriously?"

Taciana: "Warrick, do remember what Mom told us? Practice makes perfect."

Warrick: "Yeah, but that was years ago."

Taciana: "It still applies in the present. Have a goodnight, Warrick."

Warrick: "You too little, sis."

Taciana and Jackson go their separate ways.

Taciana: "Goodnight, sweetie."

Jackson: "Goodnight."

.......At 10:30 am in the morning.......

Jackson: "So Tacci, I was wondering since we aced every test, perhaps we could go catch a movie?"

Taciana: "Babe, we have to prepare our speeches for the graduation ceremony before Wednesday of this week."

Jackson: "You mean like the speech a valedictorian makes?"

Taciana: "Precisely. Think about the announcements they will make about us after we walk out on that stage."

Jackson: "We, and all of our friends, are exempt, Tacci. Therefore, we do not have to take the final exams. Besides, I am more of the impromptu speech kind of guy."

Taciana: "I know Jackson, but if we are to become the valedictorians of Wild Eye High School, then we need to write down our speeches and memorize them easily before the day of graduation."

Jackson: "Okay, we will do it the right way."

Taciana: "Hey, don't be nervous. We will get through this together."

Jackson: "Alright, let us start practicing then."

.......6 hours later.......

A knock on the front doors is heard just as they finished practicing for their graduation speeches.

Jackson: "I'll get it this time."

He goes down the stairs and opens the front doors revealing Sophia and her little sister Tia.

Sophia: "Hi Jackson, we stopped over for a little."

Tia: "I can't wait to hear the fun planned for today, Mr. Jackson!"

Jackson: "Hehe, alright squirt."

Tia: "I beat Sophie in a race back home."

Jackson: "Really?"

Tia: "Is it fun time now, please?"

Jackson: "You bet, kiddo."

Tia: "Wait, I want to shake Ms. Taciana's hand. Okay, go ahead."

Taciana: "Pleasure to meet you officially, little Tia."

Tia: "Nice to meet you too. Do you want to come and join us for story time?"

Taciana: "Sure, sweetie."

Tia: "Terrific!"

Taciana: "She is so adorable Sophia."

Sophia: "Girl, she is always a handful."

Jackson: "Reminds me of my youth, enjoying a story circle."

Taciana: "What was that like back when you were human?"

Jackson: "I always paid attention and clapped after the book ended; but I was only three when that happened."

Sophia: "You must have been a real cutie."

Jackson: "Hehe, not really."

Sophia: "I doubt that."

Taciana: "Ahem!"

Sophia: "Sorry."

They head to the living room where Tia skipped ahead. As Jackson turns the corner, he is surprised to be tackled by Tia.

Tia: "Boo!"

Tia: "I scared you three!"

Sophia: "Yes, you surprised us, little sister."

Tia: "Mr. Jackson, what happens next?"

Jackson: "Now what would you like to do, Tia?"

Tia: "Can we watch a movie?"

Jackson: "Sure."

Tia: "I wanna watch The Glumpy Fish."

Jackson: "If that is what you want."

Taciana: "Sit in my lap, Tia."

Tia: "Do you have a music machine? Your fur is so soft."

Taciana: "Of course I do. Perhaps I'll show it to you after the movie, okay? And thank you, Tia."

Tia: "Who else is coming to watch?"

Taciana: "It's only going to be the four of us for movie night."

Sophia: "I will carry you if you fall asleep."

Tia: "I won't be sleeping. I am a night wolf."

Sophia: "Hehe, we'll see about that."

The movie came to an end and Tia was lying down fast asleep on the floor.

Sophia: "Alright, little one."

Tia: "Yawnnn."

Sophia: "Thank you for the movie, Jackson."

Jackson: "Not a problem. In fact, she can have it since Tacci has outgrown it."

Taciana: "No way. It was and is still one of my favorite movies, Jackson."

Jackson: "Chill babe. I am just messing with ya."

Taciana: "Don't tease me."

Jackson: "Hehe, goodnight, Sophia."

Sophia: "Goodnight, you two."

Taciana: "So, what should we do now?"

Jackson: "Well, we are going to have to think of a new activity."

Taciana: "Hehehe, what do you have in mind?"

Jackson: "How about a crime thriller with a suspenseful theme like Authority Chasers?"

Taciana: "It is not my usual cup of tea, hun, but I will watch if you hold me close."

Jackson: "Hehehe, sounds fair."

He wraps his arm around her as she nuzzles him under his neck.

……..2 hours later……..

Saba: "Hey. You need to be asleep in a bed, and not on the couch."

Taciana: "Mom, we nodded off for a little while watching this show Jackson found. Not a big deal."

Jackson: "What's up, babe?"

Taciana: "The night police are here."

Saba: "Do not get sarcastic with me, young lady. Now march upstairs now. Jackson, out to the guest cottage. Bedtime. Both of you."

Taciana: "Alright Mom, we are going."

Jackson: "Night."

Taciana: "Goodnight."

.......Sunday Morning.......

Taciana wakes up to a phone call from Abby Squirreling.

Taciana: "Good morning, Abby."

Abby: "Hi Taciana, I need your advice about picking a restaurant with great decor."

Taciana: "I would go with the Grilled Acorn."

Abby: "Will Tobias and I like it?"

Taciana: "I am certain you and Tobias won't be disappointed, because they roast fruit and nuts on sticks."

Abby: "You mean like healthy kabobs?"

Taciana: "Exactly."

Abby: "Thanks."

.......Phone Call Ends.......

Taciana: "Abby, you lucky girl."

She looks at a photo of Jackson and walks to his cottage. Jackson is still asleep, so Taciana nudges him awake.

Jackson: "Oy vey. What's up?"

Taciana: "Jackson, wake up fully, please?"

Jackson: "Alright, you have my full attention."

Taciana: "I was thinking that maybe you and I could go on a double date later tonight."

Jackson: "With whom?"

Taciana: "Abby and Tobias."

Jackson: "Why would we do that?"

Taciana: "There will be music playing."

Jackson: "What band is it?"

Taciana: "Actually it is not a band, it is the soul artist named Tokan Kembler."

Jackson: "I do enjoy his soul music."

Taciana: "Yeah! So what do you say?"

Jackson: "I have all of his songs downloaded on my new phone, babe. So yes, of course I am coming."

Taciana: "Perfect! We'll call this our personal pre-party darling."

Jackson: "Hehe. A pre-party?"

Taciana: "Yes, a private party for the two of us before graduation. I am so excited!"

She gives Jackson a quick smooch on the mouth.

Jackson: "You enjoy that way too much."

Taciana: "I know, but you love it."

The couple head to the main kitchen and eat their toast. Ramona comes down smelling the scent of breakfast and greets them with a new attitude. She texts Martin on her phone saying that she wants them to go pick out a new car at the dealership this morning.

Ramona: "Good morning, my dear sister!!!"

Taciana: "Morning, Ramona. I take it that you and Martin were texting all night long."

Ramona: "What makes you say that?"

Taciana: "Oh come on Ramona, I am a light sleeper. Even Jackson heard you laughing when we were watching our movie."

Jackson: "She's not wrong. It was hilarious hearing all the things you were saying out loud while texting."

Ramona: "Ha Ha Ha. So what if Martin prefers texting me more than giving phone calls? It is kind of sweet actually. Oh gotta go, he just texted me saying he is outside awaiting my elegance. See you later!"

Taciana: "Well, at least we can have a peaceful morning to ourselves."

Jackson: "Couldn't agree more."

Taciana: "Hehehe. You are making me blush, hun. I hope the other couples in our group are as happy as we are."

Jackson: "They will be okay. Living with you and your family has given me the hope of a new future. Thus exuding a high amount of happiness."

Taciana: "Finding you was like finding the world's greatest treasure."

Jackson: "Now I am gonna go work out while you keep looking pretty."

Taciana watches her boyfriend walk into the private gym room as she texts Abby about the time to meet up at the restaurant.

Meanwhile at the Serpent Dealership…

Martin: "Alright Mona, here we are."

Ramona: "I appreciate you accompanying me."

Martin: "Not a problem, we are going to pick out the car of your dreams."

Ramona: "You mean it, Marty?"

Martin: "Of course. So do you have any plans after we pick up your new ride?"

Ramona: "I'm not sure."

Martin: "There is this one spot by Revonah Lake that is supposed to have a great view of the sunset."

Ramona: "Where is that exactly?"

Martin: "I don't want to reveal the location."

Ramona: "Come on, Marty. Please?"

Martin: "Okay, wise girl. I will lead the way afterwards. However, you cannot reveal the location to anyone else. This will be our regular place. Promise me."

Ramona: "Alright, I solemnly swear to not tell anyone about our spot."

.......7 minutes later.......

Ramona: "This is it!"

Martin: "You sure?"

Ramona: "I am positive that the 5020 Pixie Sidewinder is the van I want."

Martin: "Okay, I will find one of the sales assistants to give a fair price."

Ramona: "Hmm, I might just reward you with a little something in return after this."

Martin: "What's that?"

Ramona: "Hehe. I'm not sure yet. But you are going to have one happy bunny on your hands. Hehe."

Martin then informs a wolf-like sales assistant named Rufus about Ramona's decision and follows him to the open lot to pick out the model of the desired vehicle.

Martin: "Hi there, my girlfriend wants a van called the Pixie Sidewinder. Are there any more of those left in stock?"

Rufus: "Oh yes, sir. Right this way. Okay, based on how long it has been in our inventory, the cost of the vehicle is eighty thousand dollars in total."

Martin: "Excellent."

Rufus: "Will you be paying for it with cash or via credit card?"

Martin: "Actually, my girlfriend here is going to be paying for it with her credit card. I am just helping her pick one out."

Ramona: "It is truly extravagant."

She transfers eighty thousand dollars from her savings to her checking account and hands her card to Rufus.

Rufus then swipes the card in the slider part of his inventory tablet and hands it back to Ramona.

Martin: "Looks like we are traveling together in two rides to Lake Revonah."

.......50 minutes later.......

They park their cars by the empty lot near the lake and Martin tells Ramona to cover her eyes with her paws.

Martin: "Alright Mona, we are almost there."

Ramona: "How far is it?"

Martin: "Trust me, it will be worth the suspense."

Ramona: "If you say so."

.......15 minutes later.......

Martin: "Open your eyes and enjoy the view."

Ramona: "This setting is so beautiful!"

She gasped at the blue majesty of the water. He places his paw-like hands on her shoulders and massages them in a circular motion.

Martin: "I knew you would like it here."

Ramona: "Oh my goodness. Your paws feel like magic."

Martin: "Do you want to go see the waterfall?"

Ramona: "Oh yes! Eeek! What are you doing?"

Martin: "I am going to carry you into the water and chat more."

Ramona: "You don't have to do that, Marty."

Martin: "I may not be as strong as most of the furries in our school, but I am strong in spirit. I have to admit that I could never stop watching you from a distance after all these years. Even after I finished my homework alone or after a test."

Ramona: "You gotta work on your pickup lines, Marty. However, I appreciate the sentiment behind it."

Martin: "Time to dive in, cottontail queen."

Ramona: "So tacky."

The two sit down and snuggle up together on the sandy bank of Lake Revonah to watch the sunset after a nice swim.

Martin: "I am glad you talked me out of taking the final exam."

Ramona: "You are already a super genius who is exempt."

Martin: "Thanks, Mona."

Ramona: "Have you thought about ever leaving this town?"

Martin: "I have."

Ramona: "Well, I am coming with you when the day comes."

.......At the Acorn Grill.......

Abby: "Here we are, puffy cheeks."

Tobias: "I don't have puffy cheeks, Abby."

Abby: "Tobias Greenwood, your cheeks puff up every time you eat."

Tobias: "Why are you so giggly?"

Abby: "Hehe relax love, this is the Acorn Grill."

Tobias: "Let me guess, we came to try out new food."

Abby: "No Toby, I figured that we deserve at least one night to go eat out for a change."

Tobias: "Is there a special meal made out of grapes?"

Abby: "There is something even better to try as a meal, my chipmunk love."

Tobias: "What would that be?"

Abby: "A combination of any fruits or nuts of your choice. This includes honey melon, grapes, bananas, guava, cherries, strawberries, custard acorns, walnuts, chestnuts, hazelnuts, Brazil nuts, pecans, peanuts, almonds, and other assorted fruits. Quite the selection for deliciousness."

Tobias: "Okay, you have convinced me."

Jackson: "Hi there, we are here for a party of four."

Boris: "Oh yes sir, right this way."

Taciana: "Hey hey, party furries!"

Jackson: "Tobias, what's up, man?"

Tobias: "Ah, you know, waiting for the music to start."

Taciana: "Tokan Kembler should be on stage starting any minute while we wait for our drinks and food."

Abby: "Guys, there he is!"

Tokan: "Good evening everyone! How are we all doing tonight?"

Crowd: "Great!"

Tokan: "Alright, then! Here is my number one hit!"

……..Song begins……..

"I can't ride through the night without a sign,

Without your touch tonight,

The days are tested on my mind,

I've been saved by an angel of light now,

You are the one who makes my heart beat so wild that I

could fall in love again,

Standing strong with a wild, wild heart,

No more wasting time baby,

Show me what you got right now in the club tonight, with a

big wild heart."

……..As the new song continues……..

Jackson chomps on his kabob with fruit and swallows while Taciana watches Tokan busting a move on stage.

Taciana: "Come on, you three, let's shake it out!"

Jackson: "Say no more, my rabbit queen."

Taciana: "Hehe."

Abby: "Toby, don't ever let me go after this night ends."

Tobias: "Well I may drop you, if we were to do a dip while in the moment."

Abby: "Toby!"

Tobias: "Hehe I'm just pulling your chain, Abs."

Abby: "Well, be serious about this."

Tobias: "I am simply adding some humor to lighten the tone, lady squirrel."

Abby: "Just dance with me, you silly chipmunk."

The two furry couples dance in sync with the rhythmic beats of the song. Many other furries in the restaurant start making their way onto the floor and allow the music to melt their worries away.

Jackson: "What do you say, Tacci? Best pre-party ever?"

Taciana: "Yes Jacky, this is the best pre-party ever."

Tobias: "I guess those two decided to up their game."

Abby: "Come here, puffy cheeks."

She plants a long and passionate kiss on his lips until the song reaches an amiable conclusion.

Graduation Ceremony

Several hours later, the Grilled Acorn was now nearly empty after the lights went out. Tobias and Jackson are singing on stage after eating too many fruit kabobs.

Abby: "Toby!"

Tobias and Jackson continue singing one of Tokan's songs as Abby tries to get their attention.

Abby: "Are they even listening to me, Tacci?"

Taciana: "I don't know about Tobias, but Jackson is never going to stop singing until he gets it out of his system."

Abby: "Great. How long will it take?"

Taciana: "Just be patient, Abby. They are on the last song by Tokan."

Abby: "Alright, but it better be over with at some point."

.......10 minutes later.......

Tobias: "Dude, we could start our own band!"

Jackson: "What? No way."

Tobias: "No Jackson, think about it. The crowds will be cheering and begging for our autographs after every show. We could call ourselves the Furred Phoenix of Rock!"

Jackson: "That would be awesome, but we still need to have a manager sign us up for a contract."

Tobias: "Way ahead of you."

Jackson: "What do you mean?"

Tobias: "After everyone left the restaurant, I set my phone's camera to record our powerful performance."

Jackson: "We do sound good, buddy. Guess we could make it as big stars."

Tobias: "Not to mention all the moolah we'd make."

Jackson: "I see your point."

Tobias: "I guess we have a band."

Jackson: "We could add Warrick and Miles into the mix."

Tobias: "More heads are better than two!"

Taciana: "Jacky, it is time to go back!"

Jackson: "Aww come on, just one more song."

Taciana: "The sad eye routine won't work on me this time, bae."

Jackson: "Darn it."

Taciana: "Besides, our graduation is two days away."

Jackson: "Have a little faith, babe. We got this."

Taciana: "I'll show you my super-secret clothes for vacation if you are willing to practice the speech with me all day tomorrow."

Jackson: "Can we rest up after that?"

Taciana: "Yes honey, then we can rest afterwards."

Jackson: "Alright."

Abby: "We should get going too, Toby."

Tobias: "Abby, the night is still young."

Abby: "Uhhh What are you doing?

Tobias: "Giving you the face you enjoy so much."

Abby: "What face?"

Tobias: "My famous superstar face."

Abby: "Hehehehe, okay."

Tobias: "We'll get plenty of rest and prepare for our valedictorian speeches. You happy?"

Abby: "Thank you for saying that. Hehe, for a moment, I thought you were going to complain about this and not take responsibility."

Tobias: "Come on Abby, the food was great, and I rocked the night with my band."

Abby: "Ahem. What else?"

Tobias: "I will maintain a high level of responsibility."

Abby: "Good. This is good practice once we are in college and then become working adults."

Tobias: "Whoa, whoa, you are already looking into the future?"

Abby: "Yes, of course I am! I mean, we are going to mate eventually."

Tobias: "My sweet squirrel."

Abby: "My handsome chipmunk."

Tobias: "Abs, you know I would do anything for you."

Abby: "I know. I'm driving."

Tobias: "Why can't I drive?"

Abby: "You might pass out from partying too much and I don't want you to crash your car."

She kisses his cheek and drives them back to Tobias' house.

Mrs. Greenwood: "Tobias Greenwood, you were out too late past your curfew! It is 2:00 am in the morning!"

Tobias: "Mom! Graduation is practically tomorrow! The curfew doesn't even apply anymore."

Mrs. Greenwood: "Don't back sass me, young furry. Now march upstairs now. You're lucky your father is asleep at the moment."

Tobias: "Fine."

Abby: "Hi Mrs. Greenwood, I apologize for Toby being late."

Mrs. Greenwood: "No. It is not your fault, Abby. My son always wanted to be party master when he was little and he's just acting out a lot more than usual. I know you like my son, but promise me that you will make sure he doesn't cause any chaos as a furry in college."

Abby: "I promise, Ma'am."

Mrs. Greenwood: "Thank you."

Abby: "I'm going to cheer him up before I go."

She walks upstairs and opens the door to Tobias' room and jumps on the bed.

Tobias: "Not now, Abs."

Abby: "Aww poor baby."

Tobias: "Nothing is going to cheer me up."

Abby: "Not even my blissful eyes?"

Tobias: "Okay, okay. That worked."

Abby: "Hehe, dream of being the manly furry I fantasize about, Toby boo."

Tobias: "Challenge accepted."

She holds his cheeks and plants a kiss before they wish each other a peaceful slumber and she leaves.

.......Two Days Later.......

All the high school graduates Wild Eye High in Glassbec have been itching for graduation and they gather at the school stadium awaiting their diplomas. A large polar bear furry walks up on stage and makes an opening announcement for the crowd.

Principal Rendernan: "Attention Wild Eye High School! How are you all doing today?"

The students cheer with great enthusiasm for the celebration.

Jackson: "This is going to be great, isn't it Tacci?"

Taciana: "It sure is, Jacky! Thank you for keeping your promise."

Jackson: "I told you we would be prepared for this moment and here we are. I still find it amazing that there is more than one valedictorian here."

Taciana: "What can I say? So many worked hard this year!"

Principal Rendernan: "First, I wanted to thank you all for the amazing school year we've had. I'm proud of you all for helping build Flats for Furries and I look forward to helping with the summer fundraiser you are doing to help stop bullying in our hallowed halls. Now, we'll have our valedictorians walk up here and give a speech before we hand out diplomas."

Jackson: "That is our cue, bae. Come on."

The pair walk up to the stage along with the other valedictorians of Wild Eye High,

which include all of their friends.

Valedictorians: "Ahem, we are proud to accept this great honor and hope that you will continue to achieve great things in life while continuing your education as an example for furries around the world. Also, give it up for our instructors, since we'd be completely lost without them."

The entire stadium cheers out after the inspirational speech from Jackson and his group of friends. Shortly afterwards they received their diplomas and waited for the whole school to finish up.

.......6 hours later.......

All the high school graduates walk outside to be greeted by their family members to have their pictures taken and say farewells to fellow students who they may or may not see again before heading home.

Jackson: "Well Tacci, I have to admit that it has been an interesting school year."

Taciana: "Babe, you've only been here for 6 months and you still became a top scholar. That is what I call a miracle through hard work."

Tawny: "Yeah! We did it!"

Serena: "Oh yes! I can't wait for our Rabeau family vacation!"

Jackson: "That is awesome. I'm so glad your parents invited me. But when is the trip?"

Taciana: "We are flying there tomorrow via our family jet."

Jackson: "You all go on a private jet?"

Taciana: "Oh yes, Jacky. Public planes are much too slow."

Warrick: "Yeah and with our jet we'll make it there in under 10 hours."

Renet: "Will there be any spas over there, War?"

Warrick: "Yes, this time there will be a spa for you to relax in while Jackson and I go hang gliding.

Ramona: "Can we invite Martin on the trip?"

Martin: "Um, actually Mona, my parents want me to stay and enhance my scientific skills."

Ramona: "What?"

Martin: "I know, but I really just want to rest my head for a while."

Ramona: "Then come with me, Marty. I need my strong coyote furry. Otherwise, I will feel so lonely and bored."

Martin: "You are really cute when you try the guilt trip thing, but okay I will go for you."

Ramona: "Yay! We are going to have so much fun!"

She brings him to both sets of their parents to ask their permission for Martin to accompany her and they all agree to let him tag along.

Taciana: "So which island are we going to this time?"

Saba: "Oh don't worry about that too much, dear. Your father is keeping that as a surprise when you wake up after the long flight."

Taciana: "I won't fall asleep during the flight this time, Momma."

Saba: "You have said that for the last three years and you still did it anyway, sweetie."

Taciana: "Well, not this time. I swear that I will catch sight of the island before Dad can say its name."

Jackson: "Chill, my lovely rabbit, I will keep a lookout for the island in case you do fall asleep."

Taciana: "Hehehe, thank you, Jackson, I knew I could count on you.

Jackson: "I will always be there for you, scouts honor."

Taciana: "You were a Boy Scout during your time as a human?"

Jackson: "Of course, but I will tell you more about that once we reach our vacation island."

Taciana: "Okay, deal. This is going to be fun, love!"

Jackson: "Save the excitement for later, my dazzling queen."

Taciana: "I like that name, my adorable dhole."

Jackson: "This will be a trip we shall never forget."

Warrick: "Got that right, bro man."

Epilogue: Family Vacation

They fly the very next day to the Ethereal Isles on the family jet and land on their private airstrip. Bolton then leads the group to the prepaid vacation spot.

Bolton: "Welcome to Isla Kalma, everyone."

Jackson: "This place looks awesome!"

Taciana: "I knew you'd love it."

Jackson: "Is that special surprise still coming?"

Taciana: "Hehe, of course the surprise is still coming."

Jackson: "Will it happen after a day of exploring?"

Taciana: "You are going to have to keep guessing, darling. Now come and help me start unpacking."

Jackson: "Alright."

He begins placing his clothes in the drawers while Taciana sets up her grooming supplies. The day continues with everyone else setting up shop in their own hotel rooms.

.......Meanwhile in Martin's Room.......

Martin: "Extra clothes? Check. Personal Supplies? Check. Party gear? Check. Okay Mona, we are ready to get the rest of this day rolling!"

Ramona: "You are finally done, super genius?"

Martin: "Oh Mona, Mona, Mona."

Ramona: "What?"

Martin: "It is always good to double check if we have everything with us beforehand."

Ramona: "Hehe. Okay, you are right Marty. Now can we go for a swim? I heard Mom and Dad talking about hosting a family feast later tonight at 9:30 pm."

Martin: "Say no more, bunny girl. Let's splash!"

He takes her paw and they run down to the beach for a long swim.

Tawny: "What are we supposed to do here seeing as there are not that many furry boys around on this island?"

Serena: "We could go try surfing."

Tawny: "Are you serious?"

Serena: "Why not? It is not like we have anything else to do except go into town and see what locals have in store."

Tawny: "Fine."

The pair walk up to a concession stand and ask the seller for two surfboards. Serena pays ten dollars for the surfboards rental.

Surfboard Seller: "Enjoy your day."

Serena: "You remember how to do this?"

Tawny: "Sort of. I can do this. I can do this."

She stands up and tries to catch the wave, but it ends up wiping her out into the water.

.......30 minutes later.......

Tawny is found unconscious on the beach right next to her surfboard and Serena comes off of her wave to check on her.

Serena: "Tawny! Wake up! Oh no! Come on, please wake up! Sister?"

Serena runs over to the hotel and knocks on Taciana's door. Jackson opens it.

Serena: "You two have to help me!"

Jackson: "What's wrong, Serena?"

Serena: "Tawny's not breathing!"

Taciana: "Calm down, sis. Take us to her."

They run to Tawny's unconscious body.

Jackson: "Uh oh."

Serena: "Can you help her?"

Jackson: "Never fear. I am certified in CPR, Serena."

Taciana: "What should we do?"

Jackson: "Okay, first I have to check for a pulse and start performing chest compressions until she is breathing again. You two have to find a towel to keep her core body temperature warm."

Taciana: "Okay, Jacky. Please save my little sister."

Jackson: "I've got this Tacci."

When they go off searching for a comfortable towel, Jackson completes numerous chest compressions.

Tawny: (coughs up water)

Tawny: "Uggh, what hit me? Jackson?"

Jackson: "Hey Tawny, you gave your sisters a fright."

Tawny: "Were you worried, or did you do it because Taciana told you to?"

Jackson: "I saved you because I was worried I might lose my future sister-in-law."

Tawny: "Oh well, thanks Jackson. I take back what I said before about my sister's relationship with you."

Jackson: "Thanks Tawny, that is mighty noble of ya."

Taciana and Serena bring the requested towel to Tawny and hug her in relief of her current condition.

Taciana: "Oh my goodness. Tawny! Are you alright?"

Serena: "We thought you were gone."

Tawny: "I am fine. I'm alive and breathing, my sisters."

Jackson: "Anyways, let's have some fun swimming at the pool instead."

The Rabeau sisters cheered at that and followed Jackson back to the island's hotel.

Jackson: "It's party time, furries!"

Many other teens furries join in or around the pool to make some noise and get down with the music.

.......Further down on the Kalma Beach.......

Martin and Ramona are done swimming and start dancing together near the watery shoreline. They play up some tunes from Martin's music speaker.

.......4 hours later.......

Martin: "Ramona, I couldn't imagine any moment that's better than this."

Ramona: "Yeah, being out here with no one else around is like heaven to me."

She wraps her arms around his neck as Martin holds her waist while swaying to the song's harmonic beats flowing through their souls. They stare into each other's eyes.

Then an unusually big wave washes them down into the wet sand.

Ramona: "Hahahahaha!"

Martin: "Hahahahaha!"

Martin: "Now that was a hardcore splash, Mona!"

Ramona: "Hehe. Yeah, it sure was Marty, but we have to go shower before the big dinner. Follow me smooth operator; we might take in some sights along the way back."

The couple trek back to the Kalma hotel.

.......At the Kalma Suites.......

Jackson: "Are you all ready to rock and roll, party furries?"

Crowd: "Wooo! Yeah!

Jackson: "Time to dive."

Taciana: "That is my dhole."

Renet: "Isn't he kind of a showoff?"

Taciana: "My Jacky is just being himself and that is what I love about him. He shows little to no fear."

Renet: "You are a lucky girl."

Taciana: "I know."

Renet: "I am glad that Warrick is not about to try diving. He wants to keep his hair looking slick. Hehe."

Taciana: "I know my brother and he will do anything to make you happy."

Renet: "So the hair thing is just his way of saying he cares a lot?"

Taciana: "Yeah girl, he knows you don't like swimming so much."

Renet: "I think I might surprise him with something tomorrow."

Warrick: "Surprise me with what?"

Renet: "Did you hear us the whole time?"

Warrick: "When I came back with the last of the berry punch for all of us I only heard half of the conversation."

Renet: "Oh goodness!"

Warrick: "Chill baby, I will still be surprised as you reveal the gift. Also, it is almost time for our vacation dinner."

Taciana: "I will go get Jackson away from his adoring fans. Jackson!"

Jackson: "Yeah!"

Taciana: "It is time for dinner!"

Jackson: "The food is done already?"

Taciana: "Yeah, come on, Jacky!"

Jackson: "One moment, bae. I'll see you tomorrow guys!"

Taciana: "I cannot believe I fell in love with a glory hound."

Jackson: "Oh Tacci, that really hurts."

Taciana: "Jacky, a dinner on the first day of vacation has been my family's tradition for generations. I want Serena to accept you as one of us and not as a potential partner."

Jackson: "Wait, I thought your sister Serena was okay with us being together?"

Taciana: "She puts on a good act, Jackson, but it's only a ploy to get to you."

Jackson: "Whatever she has planned, it is not going to ruin what we have and our vacation."

Taciana: "Really?"

Jackson: "Call it a guarantee, milady."

Taciana: "Thanks, baby."

The four head to the main dinner table in the hotel restaurants with Saba and Bolton at the center of the table.

Saba: "Welcome everyone to the traditional Rabeau dinner."

Bolton: "I will begin the prayer to the spirit of light to protect us before we consume the feast prepared for us."

Everyone sits quietly.

Bolton: "Great and mighty spirit of light, guard us from the terrors of this world and watch over those in need as we continue our support for every charity in all corners of this greener earth."

Saba: "That was perfectly done, dear."

Bolton: "I have been saving it for a special occasion."

Saba: "Hehe."

Jackson: "I propose a toast to a new life, friendship, love, family, and future success!"

Taciana: "Bravo baby!"

Warrick: "Nailed it!"

Renet: "Hehe!"

Tawny: "Took the words right out of my mouth!"

Martin: "This super genius agrees!"

Ramona: "Yeah to all of us!"

Bolton: "Here, here."

Saba: "To a grand vacation!"

Taciana: "Happy vacation, Jackson."

Jackson: "Happy vacation, Taciana."

They share a heartfelt kiss before digging into the food on their plates accompanied by the laughter and conversations of their family and friends.

What Happened?

Jackson is sleeping when the doorbell rings. Yawning he sits up and sees the TV playing his favorite anime, Funny Furry Friends. The doorbell rings again and he sighs.

Jackson: "Because this day couldn't get any worse, I don't even get to nap? HOLD ON! I'M COMING!"

Walking through the living room, Jackson stubs his toe and hops towards the front door.

Jackson: "Stupid chair. Stupid doorbell. Stupid day."

Jackson flings open the door. Standing there in front of him is a smiling girl, looking at him nervously.

Jackson: "Oh. Back to turn me down again, Taciana?"

Taciana: "I'm sorry, Jackson. I thought I'd better explain. You rushed right out of the lunchroom when I said I couldn't go to prom with you. But I wanted to explain why."

Jackson: "Let me guess, you don't go out with nerds?"

Taciana: "No, that's not it at all, Jackson. I think you are really cool. It's just… it's just… well, nevermind. You wouldn't understand. See you later."

Jackson: "How do you know I wouldn't? Just tell me."

Taciana: "Okay… well, every year my family signs up and agrees to build houses for those who need them but can't afford them. Our weekend to help build happens to be the same as prom."

Jackson: "So you are giving up prom to go build houses for someone you don't even know?"

Taciana: "Yeah. It's really fun actually. And I like helping others. It makes me feel good inside. Anyway, I came over here to explain why so you wouldn't be mad at me. Maybe we could get together some other time."

Jackson: "Well… you maybe want some help building them?"

Taciana: "Really?"

Jackson: "Yeah. I mean… I think I could do it. And it might be fun. Helping others is always good."

Taciana: "We will pick you up on Saturday morning then! Wear work clothes."

Jackson: "I will. See you later, Taciana."

Taciana: "Actually, call me Tacci. All my friends do."

Jackson: "Alright. Cool. See you."

Taciana runs off and Jackson goes back inside. He watches the TV for a few seconds.

Serena: "No, me!"

Ramona: "That's not fair!"

Tawny: "It's myyyyy turn!"

Shaking his head at how those three never stop arguing, Jackson shuts off the TV.

Jackson: "Boy, that was a crazy dream. I'm actually kinda glad I woke up. I think even though I love that show, I don't want to be in it. I'd rather be a real-life hero helping others, than a cartoon one. Now… work clothes. Let's find some work clothes."

The End.

Falling for a Furry

www.ingramcontent.com/pod-product-compliance
Lightning Source LLC
Chambersburg PA
CBHW070223030726
47505CB00006B/1793